PRAISE FO

Little Blue Room

'*Little Blue Room* is a strident
contest between adultery and
age, is cannily watched. – *Times Literary Supplement*

'Fluent and well plotted.' – *Books and Bookmen*

'Written with gaiety and wit.' – *Glasgow Herald*

The First of All Pleasures

'Miss Maclaren evinces a proper horror of family gatherings; and
her portrayal of the incompetence of office life has enough fantastic
ramifications to convince completely.' – *New Statesman*

'A wickedly observant novel. A winner.' – *Sunday Mirror*

'I liked it immensely. The characters come tumbling off the pages,
extremely individualized and real. I was particularly impressed
by the author's ironic humour and her peculiar brand of sadness.'
– Susannah York

'I must congratulate you on an excellent novel.' – Livia Gollancz

Your Loving Mother

'Light, witty and observed with an acid bite.' – *Daily Mirror*

'Brilliantly observed, earthy and hysterically funny. It will make you
laugh even while you're groaning with sympathy.' – *Woman's Realm*

Dagger in the Sleeve

'In recent times historical novels have been few in the paperback lists.
Let us hope that *A Dagger in the Sleeve* marks a return to a genre that is
both instructive and entertaining.' – *Irish Press*

Villa Fleurie

.

By the same author
Dagger in the Sleeve
The First of All Pleasures
Ménage à Trois
The Single File
Your Loving Mother

DEANNA MACLAREN

Villa Fleurie

To the gorgeous
witty, sexy Emma
love
Deanna
x

PETER OWEN
LONDON AND CHESTER SPRINGS, PA, USA

PETER OWEN PUBLISHERS
73 Kenway Road, London SW5 0RE

Peter Owen books are distributed in the USA by
Dufour Editions Inc., Chester Springs, PA 19425-0007

ISBN 978-0-7206-1316-2

© Deanna Maclaren 2008

All rights Reserved.
No part of this publication may be reproduced in any form or by any
means without the prior permission of the publishers.

A catalogue record for this book is available from the British Library.

Printed and bound in Great Britain by
Windsor Print Production Ltd, Tonbridge

'Tennessee Waltz'
Words and music by Redd Stewart and Pee Wee King
© Copyright 1948 Acuff-Rose Music Inc., USA
Cinephonic Music Company Ltd
Used by permission of Music Sales Ltd
All rights reserved. International copyright secured.

'Goodnight Sweetheart'
Words and music by Ray Noble, Jimmy Campbell and Reg Connelly
© Copyright 1931 Campbell Connelly and Company Ltd
Used by permission of Music Sales Ltd
All rights reserved. International copyright secured.

'Sugartime'
Written by Odis Echols and Charlie Phillips
© 1956 MPL Communications Inc./Melody Lane Publications,
Inc./Peermusic (UK) Ltd
Used by permission.

To Nick Kent
with thanks for all your loving support

Acknowledgements
With many thanks to the following friends for their insights into Cannes, seafaring and the 1950s: Chuck Guest, Madeleine Blanchet, Sarah and Brian Bush, Jill and Steve Jones, Lisa Panter, Sebastien Simeons-Panter, Tim Williams, Ann Smiley and Wes, John Craig and Jill Shepperd.

ONE

London, May 1959

Patric Ryan made his move at 2.51 p.m. precisely. Paula remembered the time and the shock he caused, because when it happened she was thinking about haggis.

Paula was accustomed to business lunches and charming potential clients, but meeting Patric had been unsettling right from the start. It hadn't helped that on the way there she had argued with the taxi driver about the route he was taking, so he had stopped the cab next to a lagoon of drain water in Piccadilly. As a result, she had arrived at Fortnum and Mason's fourth-floor restaurant with sopping feet in her new court shoes.

Moving through the throng of discreetly elegant women in twin sets and pearls Paula wondered why a city-based publisher would feel comfortable here. But, as she was led to his table and saw the bevy of waitresses, she realized he must be a regular.

He stood up. As they shook hands Paula did the usual assessing. She saw tall, dark. Strong blue eyes, impeccable suit, grey silk tie, nice hands.

She hoped he approved of her – glossy black hair, blue eyes, petite, curves under control in a smart navy suit.

'I always come here for the roast beef,' he said. 'Best in London.'

Under the table Paula eased off her sodden shoes while he gave the order and asked for a bottle of Morgon. It happened to be her favourite.

Smiling, she slid into her practised potential-client routine. 'I've been cooking business lunches for City clients for ten years now, Mr Ryan. I did my initial training at catering college after the war and . . .'

He was looking into the distance. Bored.

She hurried on, 'And then I did a Cordon Bleu course in the south of France.'

The blue eyes were suddenly focused on her again. He said, 'When you were in Nice, did you learn how to use the phone – speak to the operator, do all the numbers in French?'

Hasty reassessment. Paula had not said where in the south of France she had done her course. But he knew it was Nice. Like he knew her favourite wine. Like he had checked up on her, as someone with his lawyer's training would. She had done her homework, too, but that was easy because he was in *Who's Who*. She knew he was forty. French mother, Irish father. Law degree, articled. Switched to publishing. Divorced, no children. Addresses in Chelsea and Cannes. Clubs: White's and Chelsea Arts.

And now for some reason he wanted to know if she could use a French phone.

'Yes. I had to telephone my mother.'

'What about your father?'

'Died. Air raid.'

Lunch arrived. Spreading the white damask napkin across the folds of her circular skirt, Paula wondered where the hell the conversation was supposed to go from here.

'I suppose we ought to be drinking champagne,' Patric said. 'Celebrate your book contract.'

That's fast intelligence, thought Paula. She'd signed the contract only yesterday. Dreading the whole project actually. She'd never done a recipe book before. 'Mr Ryan, if this lunch is to try to get me to switch publishers, I'm sorry, but I really can't . . .'

'No, no. Well, of course, Ryan Publishing would be delighted to have you, but we can't poach. How did the book project come about, by the way?'

'Oh, I cooked for a book launch. Just simple stuff, but I had some Caribbean food, and we put on calypso music, and now I've got to do a book of international recipes.'

He laughed. 'You'd rather not?'

It wasn't just creating the recipes, Paula explained. The publisher wanted background, colourful writing on all the countries. 'I'm a cook, Mr Ryan, not a real writer.'

He leaned forward. 'Tell you what. Why don't you write the book in the south of France? Get away from this filthy weather.'

'Where in the south of France?'

'Cannes. My villa. I won't be using it for a few months. And there's a good library you could use.'

Paula stared at the dark-haired man. He wanted to lend her, a woman he had only just met, his villa, so she could write a book for a rival publisher.

Before she was able to pose the question he did it again. Changed tack. 'Do you remember Ilona Dunbar?'

'Of course. I was at school with her.'

'I know you were, Miss Montgomery. Did you like her?'

Damn it. How did he know whom she'd been at school with? And why did it matter? Paula said, 'She always had to explain about that name – how to say it. She was very patient. No, not Ilona as if you were feeling ill but Ilona as if it's the Isle of Wight.'

'Did you like her?'

'Ilona was very popular. Blonde, sporty –'

'Did you like her?'

'I lived with the Dunbars. I was an evacuee.'

He was regarding her steadily. She could see there was no getting out of it.

'All right. She stole my boyfriend,' Paula laughed, 'but we got over it. Stayed in touch till a few years ago.'

Patric Ryan said nothing. Just looked at her. Paula felt propelled into saying, 'It was just . . . just a girlish crush I had on Hans.'

'This is the Hans that Ilona eloped with?'

Paula nodded. 'He was just very rich then, not the multi-millionaire he is now.'

'Was. He died recently. I'm the family lawyer. Arranged the funeral. Very private. Now the beautiful widow is staying at my villa. She needs people around her she can trust. She asked me to find you.'

Paula glanced at her watch. Two fifty. 'Can I call you tomorrow? There's a recipe I've got to test this afternoon.' Haggis. She'd spotted some in the food hall on the way in.

As the waitress cleared the table Patric signalled for the bill. 'It would be nice for Ilona to have a girlfriend. An old chum around the place.'

Whether it was the Irish lilt or a genuine change in the tone of his voice as he said 'Ilona', something prompted Paula to ask, as she reluctantly wriggled on her still wet shoes, 'Are you in love with her, Mr Ryan?'

He paused. 'Not now. It was just a –'

'Youthful crush?' Paula said, amused. Then, thinking she'd gone too far, she composed her features and mentally returned to her recipe. What veg went with haggis?

That was as far as she got. In a swift, decisive movement Patric Ryan reached across the table, grabbed her by the hair, pulled her towards him and kissed her. Passionately.

Fortnum's restaurant ground to a shocked halt. Waitresses froze. Dowagers' jaws dropped. The twin-set brigade stilled their pudding spoons and watched and watched until, finally, the kissing couple separated.

Pink-cheeked, Paula busied herself with gloves and handbag. 'Was that anything to do with whether or not I go to the villa?'

'No. Quite separate.'

'Will you be at the villa while I'm there?'

'Not unless I'm invited.'

'I'll telephone tomorrow. And thank you for lunch.'

On the Formica kitchen worktop in Paula's flat were a brace of haggis, a bunch of carrots, three cookery books, a stopwatch, a notebook and a scribbled message from her boyfriend Ben saying that he wouldn't be coming round tonight. Again. And it was still raining.

When the phone rang she ran into the hall, willing herself to stay calm, not to shout at Ben, be calm, sweet, so he would come round later or tomorrow.

She picked up the handset. 'Trafalgar three five seven.' Damn. Her voice was shaking.

'I want to fuck you,' said Patric Ryan.

Paula took a deep breath. Why wasn't it Ben ringing up and saying that?

'Did you hear me?'

She heard the rain battering against the stained glass of her front door.

'I'll repeat it –'

'Look, I have a deadline. My mind's on haggis and whether I can use carrots instead of swedes and turnip.'

'Carrots are perfect. Put them on to boil, and I'll come and fuck you across your kitchen table.'

'I haven't got a kitchen table.'

'I'll *buy* you a kitchen table.'

'For God's sake!'

'OK. Tell me you'll go to Cannes.'

'Look, as I'm sure you know, I'm not getting paid a lot for writing this book and I need –'

'I'll pay you double your usual fee.'

'Oh, I can't ask Ilona for money!'

'She's not paying you. I am.'

'That makes for a very expensive kitchen table.'

'Fair enough. But there is something else I want you to do for me at the villa. There is what the Yanks call an "additional agenda". Come out to dinner with me, and I'll talk you through it.'

'No.'

'Boyfriend?'

'Maybe. And you're not safe in restaurants.'

'Paula Montgomery, you kissed me back.'

It was still raining when Paula picked up the post from the hall the next morning. Just one letter, in strong, stylish handwriting she didn't recognize. One page. A poem she didn't recognize either. Four lines:

(The Lover in Winter Plaineth for the Spring)

O Western wind, when wilt thou blow
That the small rain down can rain?
Christ, that my love were in my arms
And I in my bed again!

(Anon.)

18

TWO

I̤T WAS STILL raining as Paula's plane took off for Nice. Ben hadn't rung. But what Patric had told her – at her insistence over the phone not over dinner – made her realize that Ilona did need someone to keep an eye out for her. What Patric had called a 'watching brief'.

He told her that after Hans's funeral Ilona had asked Patric to read all Hans's papers and diaries, the personal side of what had been a dynamic life. As one of Germany's richest industrialists Hans had been adept at keeping out of the public eye; 'But there's a lot to come out. A story to tell,' Patric said. 'So, depending on the sensitivity of the material and, of course, Ilona's wishes, I'll either do damage limitation as her lawyer or publish a book.'

'Isn't there still too much anti-German feeling in Blighty?' Paula said. Although not as bad as just after the war of course, when Ilona had run off with Hans.

No, said Patric, they would publish in Germany first and wait until the climate was right for a British–American launch. He had taken all the papers to the villa, and Ilona intended to use her time there to sort through them.

'The trouble is, out of the blue and against my advice, Ilona's taken on a secretary. English. Liz.'

'References?'

'Impeccable.'

'So you want me to report back. Why don't you just fly out and see for yourself?'

'It would look too obvious. You girls together, you can chat, gossip. You'll find out more than I could. Anyway, I'd rather you invited me.'

'But it's *your* villa. You're an old friend of Ilona. You don't have to be invited.'

'This time I do. By you.'

Following her porter and her three suitcases into the arrivals hall, Paula was greeted by a plump, jolly girl waving a piece of paper with Paula's name on it.

Liz had curly reddish hair and a face, Paula observed with a pang of sympathy, that was plain. A round, freckled face with little brown eyes. It was so undistinguished it reminded Paula of making biscuits and having another ten exactly the same cooling on the rack.

Emerging into the welcome June sunshine Paula basked in the heat and told herself not to be so uncharitable. She's got a very engaging smile, Paula thought, as Liz chatted on about getting a taxi, since she didn't bring Mr Ryan's car from the villa as she wasn't sure about getting all Paula's luggage to the car park.

'I'm sure the porter –' Paula was interrupted by a terrific squeal from Liz.

'Kit!'

Liz was beaming up at one of the most handsome men Paula had ever seen: tall, auburn-haired and athletically slim, with a linen jacket slung over his shoulder. His amused smoke-blue eyes were regarding the fat girl jigging up and down in front of him.

'Liz! Lizzie. What on earth are you doing here?'

'Oh my God! Kit! I can't believe it! I'm working here for a bit. In Cannes. Oh, this is Paula Montgomery. Paula, may I introduce Christopher Rowledge.'

'Kit,' said the vision, as he and Paula shook hands.

'You were probably on the same flight,' Liz said breathlessly.

I'm sure I would have noticed, thought Paula. And I bet you were travelling First.

'Where's your luggage?' she asked.

'Had it driven down. Thought it might be fun to have the old jalopy here. Oh good. There it is.'

The old jalopy, Paula saw, was a claret-coloured Daimler gliding into an illegal parking space right in front of the arrivals hall. Liz ran up and patted it. 'Oh, you've still got the same car. Goody.'

'Let me give you a lift,' Kit said to Liz. 'Then we can talk on the way.'

How on earth does she know him? Paula wondered, as the porter and Kit's uniformed chauffeur took care of her luggage.

'Your bags are safely at the hotel, sir,' the chauffeur said to Kit.

'Good man. See you later, George.'

'Thank you, sir.'

'Now come along, Lizzie, 'Kit said. 'You in the front. I want to hear all about your French lover.'

'Oh, Kit,' Liz giggled.

As Paula slid into the leather seat, Liz turned and answered the question at the top of her mind. 'I used to work for Kit's father. The old earl. He was a real gentleman. I was so sorry when he died.'

'My brother wasn't,' Kit said. 'Got the title and the house. He never got on with the old man.'

Blimey, thought Paula. He's the second son of an earl. He's an Honourable. She wound down the window and let them reminisce. They were taking the coast road, driving past a sparkling blue sea, cream and yellow-ochre villas, their gardens lush with oleanders and roses. Roses, roses. Of course, the perfume industry was just up the road in Grasse, she knew that, but somehow she hadn't associated such a profusion of them with the Côte d'Azur. Last time she'd been here it had been February, the hills on fire with yellow mimosa (the 'winter sun', the locals called it) and the shaded gardens smothered in violets.

As they passed Cagnes Paula was thinking about a book she'd read set here. It was *The Rock Pool*, about a bunch of disaffected people having a rotten time. How could you, Paula thought, breathing the scents of the sea, the jasmine, the roses, how could anyone be seriously unhappy here?

Then she sat up, concentrated, as she heard Kit say, 'So this job, Lizzie. Where are you working?'

Liz talked about Ilona, and Paula leaned forward to start earning the money Patric was paying her. 'Tell me,' she said silkily. 'How did you meet Ilona?'

Liz laughed. 'I was in the local shop buying the paper, and she came in, and she saw I was eating a cheese baguette, and she realized it was Cheddar cheese. I mean, Cheddar's got a sort of distinctive smell, hasn't it? And she said would you mind telling me where on earth you can get Cheddar in France, so I gave her a bit of the baguette and took her to this shop I've found that sells all the English things you miss. You know, baked beans, Marmite, Heinz tomato soup . . .'

Well, thanks, Paula thought. One of her three suitcases was crammed with just such items packed on Patric's suggestion as a surprise for Ilona.

'So one thing led to another, and she heard I was looking

for a job, so that was that.' She turned to Paula. 'And how do you know Ilona?'

'She lived on the Isle of Wight, and I was evacuated there from London. It was an awful time. Humiliating. The government called it Operation Pied Piper. I was ten years old, away from my mother and in a strange place. Then all the evacuees had to line up and wait for a local family to come and choose them.'

'Christ,' Kit said. 'A kids' cattle market.'

'I was convinced no one would want me,' said Paula. 'I wasn't popular at school because I didn't have smart enough clothes – you know how spiteful little girls can be. Anyway, Ilona came along with her parents, and I'd never seen anyone like her. London kids, you know, we looked pale and peaky, but she was golden and tall, and she walked straight up to me and took my hand.'

Liz looked on the verge of tears. 'I know just what you mean about not getting picked for anything. No one ever wanted me in the team because I was too fat. When we played hockey I had to be goalkeeper to fill up the space.'

'Pay attention, Lizzie. We're coming into Cannes. I need directions.'

Paula was wondering how she'd feel, seeing Ilona again after thirteen years. She changed my life that day she took my hand and took me home with her. If she needs me now, I'm glad I came. For heaven's sake, how can you not be glad you're here? she thought as they drove past the harbour gleaming with yachts, past the pretty old town on the hill and on towards the end of Cannes populated by the oldest and most beautiful villas.

Then Kit swung the car right, through open gates and up a long, palm-shaded drive. They had arrived at the Villa Fleurie.

THREE

'GOOD LORD,' SAID Kit. 'It's got battlements.'

It was indeed like a small castle, but there was nothing militaristic about the house. The Villa Fleurie was built of russet-tinted stone, with white geraniums cascading from the castellated bedroom balconies. From the south front a lavender-bordered path led down to the swimming pool, where there reclined deckchairs – the exact pink of the oleanders – along with tubs of marguerites and a rush basket heaped with towels. Another path, edged with rosemary, led to the terrace where lemon trees in huge terracotta pots guarded the double french doors.

From the terrace Paula noticed what looked like a sizeable kitchen leading on to a jasmine-shaded pergola. Under the pergola there was a large table laid with a white cloth and a promising assortment of glasses.

Perfect, thought Paula. Just perfect. Patric, you lucky beast.

And there was Ilona running from the kitchen. A white dress, her golden hair in a pony-tail, bronzed arms open wide as she rushed to embrace the dark-haired girl. 'Paula! Oh God, it's good to see you.'

Laughing, they looked into one another's eyes. And Paula thought, It's all right. It's the same as it was. It's going to work.

Then Ilona went very still and her eyes flashed sapphire blue. Paula knew that look. It meant Ilona wanted something. Or someone.

'Let me introduce you,' Paula said, feeling that, actually, formalities were unnecessary since Ilona was looking at Kit as if she'd known him all her life, and he was smiling at her with a slightly diffident charm that Paula found utterly devastating. Damn, thought Paula. There wasn't that look in his eyes when he smiled at me.

He turned to Paula, 'Let me lend a hand. Get the luggage upstairs for you.'

Oh yes, thought Paula. Come into my room. Get into my bed.

'Don't worry, Kit,' Ilona said lightly. 'The pool boy will do the bags. But you *will* stay for lunch, won't you?'

As Liz embarked on a vain search for the pool boy and ended up dragging the luggage out of the car herself, Paula watched Ilona acting as if it were an everyday occurrence to see a Daimler parked in her drive. But then in her world it was an everyday sight. Probably, at the Schloss, she and Hans had commanded a whole fleet of Daimlers.

To Paula's disappointment Kit said he'd better push on. They walked with him to the car. Kit shook hands with Ilona and Paula and opened the car door.

Oh God, thought Paula. He's going. He's going to drive away, out of our lives.

Paula and Ilona both spoke at once.

'Where are you . . .'

'Shall we . . .'

But Kit was just ahead of them. 'I tell you what. If you're free, why don't you come over and have dinner with me tonight? I'm over at Cap d'Antibes. The Eden Roc.'

Paula wondered if Ilona realized that the Eden Roc was not just the best hotel on the Cap, it was one of the most celebrated and expensive hotels in all France.

'I'd be awfully glad of your company. And, if you like, I could send my chauffeur with the car to pick you up. What do you say?'

Liz, peering round from the boot of the Daimler, was suddenly very red in the face. Heaving that case with all the baked beans probably, Paula decided.

'No, Kit, you mustn't trouble yourself with the chauffeur. I'll drive us over in Mr Ryan's car. He asked Ilona to make sure it had a good spin now and then.'

'Good. That's settled then. Cocktails at seven suit you?'

Half an hour later Paula began to unpack, taking stock of her new domain.

'Patric suggested you have his room,' Ilona had said, showing her up to the first floor. ''Cause there's a phone extension in there, so you'll be private for your business calls.'

With Ilona gone to arrange lunch, Paula laughed at the bedside phone. Business calls! Easier for Patric to ring up and talk sex to her more like.

And this was his room. Large double bed, cherrywood Provençal wardrobe, comfortable armchair, a walnut bureau that pulled down to form a writing desk. There were no photographs. The sunny, geranium-strewn terrace had just enough room for a small table and two rush chairs. He would have breakfast there, she thought. Fresh orange juice, coffee, croissants.

Suddenly hungry, Paula made her way down the marble staircase and on to the terrace. She was surprised to see the table laid just for two.

'Liz has taken a picnic to the beach,' Ilona said, lifting a bottle of rosé from the silver wine cooler. 'Tactful of her, leaving us alone to gossip.'

She poured wine for Paula and water for herself. Constanza, the maid, brought salad, olives, cheese and bread. By the time they got to the raspberries Paula had made serious inroads into the rosé and they had giggled their way through school, being Girl Guides and cheating to get their badges, cycling down those idyllic Isle of Wight lanes that led nowhere, tennis parties, meat pasties eaten on the beach, washed down with freshly made lemonade . . .

'You were always hungry,' laughed Paula. 'Always rushing in declaring "I'm starving!" and wolfing down hunks of bread and cheese.'

'Still do.'

'You don't deserve to stay so slim. I suppose it's because you don't drink.'

'Never liked the taste. And Hans wasn't a great drinker. Then the last two years he drank no alcohol, ate no food really. We had a shoal of nurses, but he liked me to be within call. He didn't want to see anyone else.'

Didn't want anyone to see him, suspected Paula. Poor guy.

'I used to go for long walks round the estate. Talk to the guards at the gate. Walk back. All my meals I had alone.'

'You should have rung me.'

'You'd moved, and I'd lost your new number. I was so glad when Patric said that he'd find you. I hope he was nice to you.'

Paula said faintly, 'I'm surprised he hasn't laid on a bit more security for you here. I know you can lock the gates but . . .'

'Oh, I couldn't stand a security guard! I hated all that at the Schloss.'

It didn't seem sensible to Paula that such a fabulously

wealthy woman should be living in such a vulnerable way. But she didn't want to sound alarmist. 'Well, if anyone tries to abduct you we'll set Liz on to them. She's got arms like a butcher, have you noticed? I bet she packs quite a punch.'

Ilona laughed. 'She's so jolly. I love having her around.'

'What exactly does she do?'

'She was supposed to help me sort Hans's papers. She speaks some German. And then she said all I needed was organizing – getting stuff into date order – so I'm handling it myself, which I really prefer. So, she runs errands, goes to the market, supervises the garden boys, drives me. I never learned to drive. Spoiled, I know.'

Lunch was over. Paula went upstairs, stretched out on the large bed and rehearsed what she would say when she reported in to Patric. It was good of him to give her the room with a phone. Patric had told her that Cannes was very proud of its modern telephone network. You no longer had to go through the operator for local calls or drag down to the post office to use a public phone. There were *cabines*, like English phone boxes. Even so, Paula was glad of the luxury of a phone by her bed. Much better than using a smelly telephone box.

The person sweltering in the phone box round the corner was Liz. She had reached boiling point. 'You bloody idiot! What do you mean, "I can send George over in the car"? We can't afford any more George. You were supposed to pay him off and send him back to drama school.'

Kit's reply was indistinct. She went on indignantly, 'And I had to offer to drive because it wasn't obvious, actually, whether I was included in the invitation.'

She heard a sort of gurgling noise. Surely Kit wasn't laughing at her? Liz clamped the phone more firmly to her ear, her face and hands running with sweat. 'And, just remember, we can only afford for you to stay three days at Eden Roc. So we've got to move fast. I must say, I think we're in with a chance. From the look on her face when she clapped eyes on you I'd say she's pretty smitten.'

Her money ran out, and Liz hung up. No point Kit knowing everything, she thought, as she left the furnace of the phone box. No point in mentioning that Paula seemed pretty smitten, too. Liz scowled as she padded back to the beach. Jumped-up bitch. I'll deal with her.

FOUR

Liz had met Kit two years before on the last night of her holiday in Le Touquet. She had first come to the area as a schoolgirl on an exchange trip. She had been looking forward to it. All her classmates had enjoyed a great time, staying out, larking about and losing you know what.

Unfortunately, the mother of the sparrow-like girl Liz was staying with had taken one look at her chubby guest and barely allowed her out. Instead, she engaged Liz in fierce conversation, and as a result Liz went home with fluent French and her virginity intact.

But after she'd started work she would come back to Le Touquet for her holidays, usually out of season. She met Kit in a casino there. Not the kind of casino frequented by bejewelled women and rich, attentive men; this was a seedy, backstreet affair, with a raffish air that appealed to Liz.

The fact is that Liz was fed up with being 'good old Lizzie' whom everyone liked but no one envied. Men liked Liz. With her ample figure, kindly public persona and love of food, she'd had several proposals of marriage. But she had resigned herself to the way the devastating men, the charmers, the ones who intoxicated women with insane lust, these men would never fall over themselves to seduce someone as plain as her. No, if ever The One came along she knew the moves would have to come from her.

Meanwhile she enjoyed her little excursions to Le Touquet and the bolthole of the casino, where most of the other women looked raddled or wrinkled or both. Anyway most of them looked worse than Liz, which was comforting.

When she first saw Kit he was working behind the bar. It featured black wallpaper with sequins stuck on. Kit had a sickly pallor, hair that looked as if he'd cut it with nail scissors, and he was nicking money from the till.

Liz knew. She just knew she had to have him. It was like a light-bulb exploding in her head. She went to the ladies' and undid the top buttons of her fitted cardigan. One asset she did have was sensational breasts. Then she sauntered back, leaned over the bar and said to him, 'I saw you.'

'What?'

'I saw you on the fiddle. What's it for – drugs or gee-gees or what?'

'Yes. No. I – I got chucked out of my digs. Couldn't pay. I've lined up somewhere else, but they want the rent ante-post.'

Sensing his confused state, Liz moved in, forcing herself to control her excitement. 'You can come back with me. I'm in a *pension*.'

He looked doubtful. Great tits. But did he want to share a room with them?

She said, 'We don't have to do anything, you know. Perhaps I could give you a massage.'

His face brightened, and under cover of the hiss of the coffee-machine she leaned close to him and told him what she intended to do.

He said, 'You'd really do that? Really?'

'Play your cards right.'

The owners of the *pension* always went to bed early and

would leave her some supper on the stove. Liz lifted the lid of the pot and saw it was navarin of lamb.

Kit slumped at the kitchen table. 'God, that smells good.'

She said, 'Wash your hands.'

He didn't move.

'Did you hear what I said?'

He still didn't move.

She kicked him on the ankle. Hard.

He washed his hands. She served supper. They went upstairs and he instantly fell asleep. In the morning she woke him up and fucked the arse off him.

Liz trotted him back to her bedsit in East Croydon, got him off the dope, controlled his drinking, made him grow his hair and dipped into her meagre savings to give him a small allowance to fritter away at some scruffy snooker hall in Streatham.

She heard his story. After his father died he dropped out of medical school and went round the world crewing on yachts. He had loved it. No responsibilities, travel, good money. And then had come the drugs and the gambling and the slide down, picking up work in bars, clubs, whatever. The inheritance from his father dwindled to nothing. He didn't care. He never cared about anything or anyone until Liz took him back to that room in Le Touquet and enslaved him.

He adored her. OK, she was no Brigitte Bardot to look at, but in his yachtie days he'd played the sun-kissed goddess field and they left him cold. Liz was dynamite, absolute dynamite in bed. The stuff she knew! He loved his life with her. He went down the snooker hall, looked in at the betting shop, watched television, took over the shopping and had a meal ready for Liz when she got home from work. He was happy, happy, happy.

Liz was not. Oh, she was thrilled to have Kit with his smoky-blue eyes and gorgeous body – he was amazingly fit considering he'd been a layabout for the past couple of years. But she wanted more. More than nine-to-five, a Chinese meal on Saturday nights and some Spanish plonk with Sunday lunch. To hell with East Croydon. She wanted to live in London, New York and the Dordogne, with spells in Gstaad, Antibes and Paris in between.

She had a vision from years back, the result of a school trip to the Solent. It was bustling with smart yachts. But then she saw *the* yacht, *her* yacht. At first, spotting the masts out at sea, she thought she was looking at two boats. Then, as it rounded the headland, she saw it was a large motor yacht, majestic yet streamlined, all gleaming white with its polished brass glinting in the sunlight. She was called the *Lady Jenny*.

Liz gripped the harbour rail, sick with longing. 'One day, that's what I'm going to have.'

Her schoolmates were convulsed with laughter, reminding Liz that the odds on winning the pools were roughly the same as being murdered. That Liz could ever marry money was, of course, not mentioned, being completely out of the question. I mean, look at her, fat old Lizzie, bulging out of her school gingham blouse.

Liz heard what they said, knew what they were thinking and never forgot the *Lady Jenny* and all she represented. It infuriated her that Kit had been part of that way of life and had squandered it. Now he didn't seem to give a toss. He was nearly thirty, for heaven's sake, and what had he hung on to? A gold watch and the car that Daimler chairman Bernard Docker had presented to the old earl when Docker was going through a phase of sucking up to the toffs. The Daimler was now on permanent loan to some spiv from the snooker hall. Kit didn't seem bothered about driving it. He went to Streatham on the bus. He had no ambition, no aspirations. He was supremely content loafing about in a bedsit in bloody East Croydon.

Despite Liz's restlessness life would probably have just drifted on if she hadn't noticed one evening that something was missing.

'Kit. Where's your watch?'

He picked up the *Evening Standard*. 'What?'

'Your watch. Your gold watch.'

'Oh. I took it off to wash up. Put it down somewhere. It'll turn up.' He turned a page.

Liz snatched the paper from him. 'You're lying. When are you going to learn? I always know when you're lying. WHERE IS IT?'

His handsome face had gone the colour of processed peas.

'Tell me!'

He swallowed. 'I – Liz, I had to take it to the pawnbroker. I, well, I put rather a complicated bet on. I mean, if it had worked we'd be in the Caribbean by now . . .'

Liz covered her face with her hands. 'How much? How much did you put on? How much have you lost?'

His reply came in a croak. 'A pony.'

'What? Who's pony?'

'No, a pony. It's betting slang. Means five hundred quid.'

She stared at him in confused disbelief. 'This is a joke, of course. I mean, you haven't got five hundred pounds. I don't have five hundred pounds. So how could you put on five hundred when it simply isn't there?'

'I borrowed it, Liz.'

'Oh, you took out a bank loan!'

He ignored the sarcasm. 'I borrowed it from Sharkey. You don't know him. He's a used-car dealer. There's a lot of money in used cars.' He disappeared into the kitchenette and came back with the bottle of Spanish red wine Liz had been saving for Sunday.

Kit poured two glasses and went on, 'Sharkey wanted his money back, of course. So I had to pawn the watch, just to give him something.'

'Bad move,' said Liz. 'It means legally you've acknowledged the debt.'

'It means, for the time being my head does remain attached to my body. Sharkey's mob don't mess about.'

Liz lit two Kensitas and passed one to Kit. 'So where are we with all this?'

The 'we' meant everything to Kit. He could stop worrying. With Liz on board everything would be all right.

'They've given me a month to get the money. I was wondering if your parents –'

'My parents live in a council house, Kit. And, in case you've forgotten, I earn eight pounds a week and the landlord is putting our rent up.' Not to mention food, fags and fares.

Kit sighed. 'OK. There is another way out, Liz. Sharkey says I can earn back the money.'

Liz frowned. Somehow the words 'earn' and 'Kit' didn't seem to go together.

He rushed on. 'They, you see, they need a driver . . .'

Light dawned. Liz sat rigid with horror, mentally scouring her wardrobe for clothes suitable for prison visiting.

'No! You are not going down that path, Kit.'

'But . . .'

'I don't know. But I'll think of something.'

For ten years, since she was eighteen, Liz had worked for a press-cuttings agency. She had a list of clients in the health-and-beauty field – Drene shampoo, Brylcreem, Odo-Ro-No deodorant – about a hundred in all. Her job

35

was to scan the papers and magazines for mentions of the product, underline the relevant paragraphs and arrange for the cuttings to be sent to the client.

In the week following Kit's confession she was so dry-mouthed with terror she could barely concentrate.

'You all right, Lizzie?' her boss enquired, dropping a batch of foreign publications on to her desk. The agency valued her. She was conscientious, and her fluent French and passable German enabled her to scan the continental papers as well as the British ones.

That was how she happened across the item reporting the death of Hans Fleig, millionaire industrialist, after a two-year illness. He was survived by his wife Ilona. There were no children. There was a picture of them both taken years before at a charity ball – Hans tall, blond, baronial; his wife ravishing in Givenchy.

Liz learned that the funeral was private. No quote from the widow, of course; just a brief statement from the family lawyer Patric Ryan. With a strange, mounting sense of excitement Liz turned to other magazines, the gossipy ones. And there it was. A short interview with the Fleigs' housekeeper, tearful that Mr Ryan 'has taken Frau Fleig away to France. Such a charming lady. She nursed him devotedly. He was the love of her life . . .'

Liz scurried to *Who's Who*. Discovered that Patric Ryan gave an address in Cannes. She pleaded a headache, went home early and found Kit lying on the sofa watching television: *Muffin the Mule*. She threw him on the floor, stood over him and announced, 'Congratulations, Kit. You're going to get married.'

Of course, she had to talk him into it. He was appalled at the plan, whereas to Liz the audacity of it was electrifying.

'OK, she's recently widowed, but Hans was seriously ill

for two years. She nursed him. There can't have been much sex. She must be desperate for it.'

Kit would, Liz declared, have an entirely new wardrobe. A new look. Out would go the jeans and sloppy sweaters he was so attached to. Instead, he was to dress mainly in classic white, sexy and sporty, playing up to his athletic body and his elegant walk. He was to look healthy and fit, in charge of his body and his life. It was an image any woman would find attractive, but it would be especially appealing, argued Liz, to a juicy young widow.

'But I don't want to marry this woman,' moaned Kit. 'I don't want to marry anyone. Marriage means kids, and I loathe children. Oh, Liz, why are you doing this?'

'You know why. We have got to get Sharkey paid and off our backs.'

'I know, but –'

'Look! If you can come up with a better plan I'd like to hear it.'

His silence said it all.

Liz slammed into the kitchenette. At least I've got the guts to go through with it. At least I'm a realist.

She suspected that sooner or later the allure of the daily round in East Croydon was going to pall for Kit. He'd want more excitement – drugs, stronger drink, faster horses. The betting shop was opposite the snooker hall. Going back on the slide like this would take money. More than Liz would, or could, give him.

There seemed to be no question of him getting a normal job. Liz could manage it. She knew the ropes. Get to the office bang on time, cheerfully agree to do anything and pretend you hadn't heard the old lags in the post room calling you the 'London Derrière'. Ho, ho.

She was sure that when Kit had been at sea he had been capable of knuckling down to shipboard discipline. Otherwise he'd have been thrown in the drink. But on dry land Kit speedily reverted to his lazy, irresponsible, impressionable self.

If I act now, Liz reasoned, I've a better chance of keeping him in my life. OK, he'll be another woman's husband, and she's much better looking than me, but she's rich. Rich, rich, rich. And she won't have him for ever. Once he's got his hands on her money Kit can disappear off her map and fix us up with a swanky apartment. Mayfair, Paris . . .

'So you can always bugger off and leave her after a couple of years, Kit.'

'She might not like me, Liz.'

She ignored this. She loved him so much she couldn't imagine any woman not falling headlong for him. She loved him enough to give a week's notice at work, collect ten years' worth of loyalty bonus and spend a large part of it on new clothes for him. She loved him enough to loan him to Ilona.

They had to do it. They had to capitalize on their assets. Kit had the looks, the family connection, the expensive education, and he could charm. She, Liz, had the organizing ability.

'We need to get going. I'll give you twenty pounds to keep that Sharkey crook at bay until we're out of the country. Then you buy clothes. You get that watch out of hock. Then get that Daimler back and drive it to the Riviera.'

It could work, Liz thought. She could sort of taste that it *would* work.

What a stroke of luck, though, about that cheese. Who would have guessed that someone as willowy as Ilona could be so obsessed with food?

When she arrived in Cannes Liz had found a cheap hotel near the Villa Fleurie and got chatting to the owner of the local shop. Yes, there was a lady at Monsieur Ryan's villa. No, he was not with her. She came herself to buy her paper and bread every day and said she must study the newspaper, improve her French. She was *charmante*.

Hanging around at the shop several times a day, Liz couldn't work out any magic plan that would get her feet under the table at the Villa Fleurie. She just hoped Ilona would say hello to a fellow countrywoman, and from then on nice Liz could find ways to make herself useful.

She'd come prepared. In her canvas shoulder bag was her driving licence and two glowing references, one from the press-cuttings agency and the other allegedly from Kit's father that they'd cobbled together on the last of his crested family writing paper. Back at the hotel were her secretarial and school certificates, including a distinction in needlework, which Kit said was as useful as having a qualification in skipping.

And at last Ilona appeared, going nuts over Liz's cheese baguette. Liz hadn't admitted that a hunk of bread and cheese was her lunch *and* dinner. She drove Ilona down the coast to the English shop. By the time they got back to the villa they were chatting like old friends, and Liz's job was in the bag. She moved out of the hotel the following morning.

Not, Liz thought now, trudging back from the beach, that it had all been plain sailing. Frying up some chips for their supper, Liz had nearly scalded herself when Ilona mentioned that she didn't drink. For heaven's sake! How bloody inconsiderate. Champagne, gallons of it, had featured large in Liz's seduction plans for Ilona.

And then she hadn't expected this old friend, this Paula, to turn up. She was all right but somewhat, kind of, superior. Still, she obviously fancied Kit. Wouldn't do Ilona any harm to sense a bit of competition.

Towards Ilona Liz felt an affectionate interest. The affection wasn't rooted in liking. It is too much to ask that women who are beautiful and rich should be liked by women who are not. Rather, Liz's warmth towards Ilona was based on the latter being amenable enough to fall in with her plans so readily.

She glanced at her watch. It was after four. With luck the spoiled bitch and the snotty bitch would have stopped reminiscing by now. If I have to listen once more to the story of how Ilona eloped with Hans I shall go screaming mad, she thought.

FIVE

'Y OU WERE SUPPOSED to ring this afternoon.'

'I know. I fell asleep.'

'What are you wearing?'

'Not much.'

'What not much exactly?'

'Bra and knickers.'

'What are the knickers made of?'

'Lace. Expensive. I don't wear cheap underwear.'

'I'll make a note. Take them off.'

'No.'

'When I take them off I shall have you lying on the bed with your legs up.'

'How sweet of you to arrange for me to be in your room. Convenient to have the phone extension for my business calls.'

Patric laughed. 'I have to be able to talk to you. I couldn't expect you to keep nipping out to a public phone to let me know what's happening.'

'Well, I don't think you've got anything to worry about viz Liz. She's very pleasant. Offered to help typing my book.'

'Good. Use the villa library for your research. It's well stocked, and there's lots in English.'

'How considerate. A library. And a phone in my room.'

'I wanted you to get used to being in my bed.'

'I'm late for dinner. We're going to the Eden Roc.'

'With?'

'Kit Rowledge. We met at the airport. He's gorgeous.'

'You haven't seen me yet. Properly.'

'I have to get ready.'

'I'm at home tonight. Can you ring when you get back?'

'We might be late.'

'Doesn't matter. I want to hear your voice.'

Paula put down the phone and reached for the black dress laid on the bed. Who exactly, she wondered, is Patric checking up on?

Waiting in the elegant salon for Ilona, Paula saw she had placed on the piano a photo of her wedding. Paula picked up the silver frame. Such a handsome couple. Such a romantic story. Damn you, Ilona. You stole him from me.

And Ben still hadn't rung.

Ilona wafted in wearing an ice-blue chiffon dress with a man's watch strapped to her wrist. 'Do you think it looks wrong, Paula? It was Hans's. I like to wear it . . .'

Paula kissed her on the cheek. 'It's a loving thing, Ilona. Leave it on.'

Liz had Patric's white convertible at the door. Ilona insisted that Paula sit in the front.

Her mind on times past, and loves lost, Paula said to Liz, 'Have you heard the story of how Ilona eloped with Hans?'

Liz nearly ploughed the car into a palm tree. Not again. Oh God, not this bloody story again.

Beaming, she turned to Paula. 'Yes, Ilona has told me, but it's so romantic I'd love to hear it again. It's like a fairy story – you want to hear it over and over.'

'Well,' Paula began as Liz took the coast road towards Cap d'Antibes, 'during the war Ilona and I lived on the Isle of Wight, and we were Guides. I was patrol leader of Chaffinch patrol, and she was patrol leader of Kingfisher. We loved it. The lanyard, the whistle . . .'

I shall throw up, thought Liz. All over the dashboard. Ruin the whole plan.

'. . . Church parade. I carried the flag. The Union Jack. It was quite complicated. There was a series of moves, of steps you had to do in certain directions, and the flagpole was heavy, though I had a leather holster . . .'

It was like one of those ghastly modern operas, decided Liz. '*I had a leather hol-ster,*' warble-warble. '*Oh, did you? How in-ter-est-ing. What happened th-en?*'

'So Ilona and I used to get to the church early so that I could practise. Well, Hans was a prisoner of war. German officer. Shot down. Sundays the officers came to church.'

'You should have seen Paula the first time she saw Hans,' Ilona chimed in. 'Nearly dropped the flag!'

'Ah well, you were the cunning one. Know what Ilona did, Liz? She left a note for Hans in his hymn book. After the next parade she sweetly offered to tidy up the church and found he'd left a note for her. Again in the hymn book. Went on for the rest of the war.'

'I was the only person who felt sad when the war ended. He was sent back to Germany. I thought I'd never see him again.'

'But he turned up and swept you away,' Liz said, trying to hurry the account along.

'Wasn't it tricky for him getting into the country?' Paula asked. 'Germans weren't exactly popular at that time.'

'Patric Ryan handled that. He was Hans's interrogating

officer. They had a lot of respect for one another and stayed in touch after the war.'

'Your parents must have been livid when Hans turned up,' observed Liz.

'Well, I was only seventeen. The only thing to do was bolt.'

Liz turned the car into the drive of the Eden Roc, past borders of lilac and pink petunias, freshly watered, and there they were, at the hotel where for many the south of France had really started. This was where Scott and Zelda Fitzgerald had come with their friends one summer. No one in 1923 visited the south of France in summer, but they did, clearing the beach of seaweed and begging the owner of the hotel to stay open for them. It was the best move the owner ever made, transforming a modest winter place into one of the most fashionable hotels in the world. One of the most famous, too, when Scott Fitzgerald used it as his setting for *Tender Is the Night*.

The bellboy came to park the convertible and they drifted on to the terrace. It was decorated in 'roaring thirties' style, with white railings and yellow cushions. Kit was waiting. He stood up. He spent so much time in East Croydon lying down Liz found it very sexy now to see him stand up for a woman.

He shook hands with Ilona and Paula and gave Liz exactly the right sort of friendly squeeze. Paula said she would have a cocktail, an Americano, and when Ilona asked for a *citron pressé* Kit said, 'Soft drink for you as well, Lizzie?'

Liz went red. Damn it, I'm paying for all this!

'No – yes, I'll have the same as Paula,' she stammered.

Concealing her amusement, Paula offered Liz a cigarette. Oh dear, I do believe our Liz is a bit sweet on Kit. Poor old Lizzie.

The drinks arrived. Liz dragged gratefully on the du Maurier and fiddled with the Americano swizzle stick, trying to control her turmoil. On the one hand, she was furious with Kit for patronizing her. On the other, when they'd walked in and she looked at him she'd nearly burst with pride. He was stunning, the linen jacket, white shirt, white trousers – total class.

When they went into dinner Liz saw that he'd had the sense to reserve a round table. He placed Ilona and Paula on either side of him. Over the perfectly chilled gazpacho he talked briefly about his job in pharmaceuticals. They had reckoned his two years at medical school would help him wing that one, and, let's face it, Liz had said, you've got to have a job. You can't say you've spent the last two years playing snooker and watching *Muffin the Mule*.

Now he was talking to Paula, encouraging her to tell him about her business. Good, nodded Liz. Don't pay Ilona too much attention. God, he looks sensational! You think so, too, Ilona, I can tell from that little moist mouth of yours. Well, your turn will come, my sweetheart. But tonight you may only look. The smoky eyes, the fine-boned face and, oh, those long wrists and sensitive hands. Imagine those hands caressing you, Ilona. And if you could see the rest of him. He's got marvellous legs. You should see him – well, you *will* see him – in those white shorts I bought him.

The waiters brought dressed lobster, a bottle of Petit Chablis and jugs of iced water. Liz was growing increasingly anxious. How much is all this costing? Kit must get out of Eden Roc in two days' time. Where can he go? Must be somewhere that looks upmarket but is cheap. He can hardly sleep on the beach. His clothes have got to look pressed . . .

'So why did you give up your yacht?' Paula was asking.

Kit's first plan had been to say he ran it aground off Antigua, but Liz said that this wouldn't convey an appropriately responsible image.

Kit said casually, 'Well, you know what they say about boats. They give you two of the greatest days in your life. The day you buy it and the day you sell it.'

Liz started to relax. Well done, Kit. Not too original, not smart Alec, delivered with endearing modesty.

'I must tell Joleen that,' said Ilona. 'Do you know them, Kit? Joleen and Colin Love. They have a boat called *Lovebite*.'

He shook his head. Frankly, he didn't imagine a bloke called Love would be allowed anywhere near the snooker hall.

'Oh, they've done so well, those two. You remember Colin, Paula. His mother ran our local tea shop. The caff, we always called it. He met Joleen after the war and went with her back to the States. They built up a fantastically successful business, what they call "fast food", and of course they called it Lovebites.'

A caravan, Liz was thinking. If push comes to shove we'll rent him a caravan. There's a site down the coast. Can't invite Ilona there, but as long as he's got the Daimler to turn up at the villa in – or, no, I've got it. Yes. A *boat*. We'll rent a little boat . . .

She went suddenly cold. Kit was touching Ilona. He was touching her wrist; admiring her late husband's watch.

'Such a romantic story,' Paula said. 'Ilona and Hans.'

No! Liz was having none of this. She could see what that rat Paula was doing, trying to give Kit a message that there was nothing doing with Ilona. 'What about you, Paula,' said Liz in her nicest, jolliest way. 'Have you got a romantic interest in your life?'

Crude but the best Liz could do.

Ilona was laughing. 'Of course she has. And I know who!'

Paula stared at her. She hadn't said a word about Ben to Ilona. Mainly because the swine hadn't telephoned.

'I'm afraid I heard you on the extension before we came out,' said Ilona.

Paula's face flamed the colour of the raspberry sorbet dominating the dessert chariot. Patric. Talking dirty. Oh God.

'It's all right. It was just the end I heard. He seems very anxious to hear from you.'

Paula looked over at Liz. Normally she would have diverted attention from herself by enquiring sweetly about Lizzie's love life, but with that piggy body what was the point? Instead she turned to Ilona. 'I'm sorry. I didn't know you were waiting to use the phone.'

'I wanted to get hold of Joleen. She'd said they were bringing the yacht into Cannes next Friday, but she hasn't confirmed. She was planning a party on board. Kit, you should come along.'

'Love to,' said Kit, 'but I'll be gone by then. Thought I'd push on. Explore a bit.'

'Well,' Ilona said, 'why not use the villa as a base? There's loads of room.'

'Oh, I couldn't possibly impose.'

'No, no, you'd be doing us a favour. Paula and Patric have been getting at me about security, and I think they're right. It would make us all feel better to have a man about the place.'

Kit raised a finger to the wine waiter. 'I think, the Château d'Yquem.'

'Isn't that Schumann you've got on? The Arabesque?'

'Yes.'

All right, she was showing off, but he could have shown a bit of admiration that she'd recognized it.

'Pleasant evening, Patric?' She meant: Are you alone?

'I'm working.'

'I'll ring off then.'

'No. Tell me what happened.'

When she got to the bit about Kit coming to stay, he said drily, 'Why am I totally unsurprised?'

'Look, he's a gentleman. Stands up at the right time.

Deals well with waiters. And he's gallant to Lizzie, which is kind.'

'Why?'

'Well, she's – she's very round.'

'You mean she's fat.'

'I had puppy fat years ago. It's not funny.' No need to tell him that Ilona's father used to call her Dumpling. Pointless handing Patric that kind of ammunition. 'And I think she's sweet on Kit.'

'And you're not?'

'Actually I have a boyfriend.'

'Racing out to join you in the south of France.'

'He's busy working.'

'I'm always busy, but it wouldn't stop me giving you the fuck of your life.'

'How modest you are.'

'I know what I'm doing. And I know what I want, Paula Montgomery.'

When she put down the phone she had to accept he made an agreeable change from the never-there Ben. Patric Ryan was an arrogant sod, but at least he *wanted* her.

The spacious kitchen at the Villa Fleurie was predominantly blue and yellow. Primrose cupboards with a dresser displaying Provençal china. There was a traditional tiled floor, a table painted dusty sky-blue, wooden chairs with rush seats and blue gingham curtains. Paula had laughed when Liz said she hated the curtains, as they reminded her of having to wear gingham at school.

They were breakfasting at the blue table in a state of girlish excitement over Kit's arrival the following day. Which room to put him in? The villa had six bedrooms. Paula was on the first floor in Patric's room. Ilona occcupied the grand main bedroom along the corridor. Liz was up on the second floor.

'Kit can have my room,' offered Paula. 'It's got a hand-basin. I can move into one of the rooms near Liz.'

No thanks, thought Liz. 'No, you need the room with the phone in.'

'For your business calls,' smiled Ilona.

Damn, thought Paula. She does know it was Patric.

'Would it be better,' Liz said, 'for Kit to have the room next to me? I know the view isn't as good as mine, but he'd be next to the bathroom. Convenient for him.'

Ilona burst out laughing. 'But, Liz, that's the old nursery. We can't put Kit in a room that's still got teddies and a golly.'

Yes we can, smiled Liz. You have no idea what I intend to do to Kit with that golly. Oh, naughty Golly! 'I don't think he'd be bothered.' Liz's mind was racing. 'It would remind him of his bedroom in the family home. His old nanny told me he always refused to move out of it. Such a shame his brother has got the house now. It was lovely.' She sighed and was pouring them all more coffee when the phone rang.

Liz went to answer it in the hall. She came back and said to Paula, 'It's for you.'

Ilona's eyebrows went up in amusement, and Paula thought, Patric, I'll slaughter you!

'It's Kit,' Liz said.

'Oh. Why does he want to speak to me?'

'I really don't know, Paula.'

As she went to the phone Liz got on with the shopping list. She was going to the market. With a man coming they had to stock up the larder.

Paula came back, fitted a cigarette into her tortoiseshell holder and lit up. 'You know, that Kit is a true gentleman. He just said to me, look, he didn't want to put you on the spot, Ilona. He knew that after a few drinks things get said and then regretted.'

'But I don't drink.'

49

'No, well, you get the drift. Basically, if you've changed your mind about him staying he quite understands.'

'What did you say?' asked Ilona.

'I asked him,' Paula was spluttering with laughter. 'I asked if he'd mind sharing his room with a golly. And he said, he said no, he'd regard it as a privilege.'

'Good.' Liz reached for the straw shopping basket. 'I wonder what Kit likes for breakfast.'

SIX

'NOT GOING?' SCREAMED Joleen. 'What do you mean we're *not going*?'

Colin wished she wouldn't screech like that. One day she'd shatter the windows and fall headlong into Manhattan. And it was especially bad that she bawled at him in front of one of the maids. The uniformed girl had gathered the remains of Joleen's breakfast coffee and juice on to a silver tray. Colin opened the door for her.

Joleen yelled, as she did every morning, 'I wish you wouldn't *do* that, Colin.'

'It's only polite.'

'It's unnecessary. Maids are trained to open doors and carry trays all at the same time.'

Colin gazed through the silk-curtained window on to the blossom of Central Park. He wished he could be in the park, on the drift, maybe meeting a pal for a drink and a laugh. He couldn't remember the last time he'd had a laugh or the last time he'd had sex, let alone the two together.

'I *said*, Colin will you stop gawping out of the window and tell me exactly what you meant about us not going.'

He took a deep breath. 'OK. The cruise is off because the crew have scarpered.'

'Scarpered?'

Honestly, thought Colin, from the snotty way she spoke you'd think she'd been educated at Vassar, not dragged up on some trailer park.

'Scarpered, Joleen. Buggered off. Jumped ship.'

Her yellow eyes glittered. It had been the first thing he'd noticed about her. Never seen a girl with yellow eyes before.

'But they were on a retainer,' spat Joleen. 'They were paid to loaf around on the boat in the south of France all through the winter. They were paid –'

'Sure. And now they've got a better offer.'

'Poached!' The amazing eyes narrowed. 'You wait, Colin Love. I shall find out who's done this. I shall ring my friends Lady Docker and Lady Kilmartin and find out and then – and then . . .'

Colin watched her splutter to a halt. One thing about his wife, she knew when she was outgunned. Just because they owned a 130-foot yacht it didn't put them in the same league as the Dockers, the Kilmartins and the Duke of Westminster, who kept their boats in Antibes if they weren't wintering in the Caribbean. If one of the big boys had stolen Colin Love's crew, well, tough; none of them was going to give a toss.

'So there we are,' Colin said, aiming for the door. 'No crew, so the cruise is off. Now I must –'

'GET ANOTHER CREW, COLIN!' Joleen was at the door, heading him off. 'We can't not go. Ilona is counting on us. When that lawyer guy rang up he said she needs her old friends with her. He's counting on us to pitch up. Ilona can't have fortune-hunters and riff-raff sharking round her. She needs old reliable friends on her own social and financial level.'

She tossed back her mane of blonded hair. Colin had

preferred it when it was fudge-coloured. Went better with the eyes.

'Besides, I've told Lady Docker we're going. If the dates match up she's going to ask us aboard the *Shemara*. So get down to your office and call the yacht crew people in Antibes.'

Colin left. He booked the call to the south of France. Then, sweating, he rang his accountant in downtown Manhattan.

From the window, Joleen watched the doorman whistle up a cab and hold open the door for Colin. She said to herself, as she said most days, I wonder what the poor people are doing today.

Then she saw one of them. A poor person, one she knew. It was her maid, starting her day off. Actually the girl didn't look down at heel; she looked sassy-smart, thanks to the blue silk dress Joleen had passed on to her. It was an odd experience, Joleen thought, seeing your clothes on someone else. Even after you'd urged the maid to take the dress, insisting it would look better on her than on you, when you saw that dress being worn it was as if the girl you'd given it to had stolen something from you.

She watched the maid dash across the road and pause on the sidewalk, unselfconsciously turning to check that the seams on her stockings were straight. Joleen smiled. At least I'm paying her enough so she can afford a pair of stockings. She hasn't got to draw a line up her legs with eyebrow pencil like I often had to.

As the girl straightened up a young man came up behind her, put his hands round her waist and whirled her round. They gazed at one another laughing, and then, with a passionate abandon, they kissed. When at last they drew breath Joleen saw the young man was carrying something. It was a hot dog in a bun. He offered her a bite and took one himself. Then they turned into the park, his arm round her waist, her head on his shoulder.

They were so young and so in love Joleen felt a sudden yearning surging through her. To be them. To have a romance like that. Oh, to be them . . .

And then she got a grip. She despised herself when she got soggy like this. Couldn't let on to Colin, of course. Joleen going soft! Colin would have a fit. 'Come on,' he'd say. 'You don't really want to be like them. Remember where you come from.' Home for Joleen had been one room above a laundry with Pop coming on to her, Mom trying to stop him and Pop belting shit out of Mom.

Joleen had been upfront about it when she got herself invited to tea with Lady Docker in London.

'Your father used to – touch you?' enquired the horrified Lady Docker.

'Just kidding around when I was young. Then it started to get serious when I was twelve. So I ran away.'

'But where to?'

'My grandmother. In Illinois. She lived in what you Britishers call a caravan and we call a trailer. She died when I was fifteen. I got a job. Waiting table.'

Yeah, thought Joleen, looking down on Manhattan. I know about poor. But what I also understand now is that it's a responsibility having money. Take this cruise. Colin simply doesn't understand how much I have to do.

She flung herself down at her inlaid walnut desk. God she hated this apartment. So old-fashioned. She wanted contemporary brights. First thing back from the cruise she'd get the designers and decorators in.

This crew fuck-up was a pain in the ass. The original crew were *trained*. Joleen had seen to it that they knew Mrs Love ate only fruit for breakfast and Mr Love did not want to see chicken at lunchtime. Joleen had personally written instructions to the skipper. The master cabin and bathroom were to be cleaned while Mr and Mrs Love were at breakfast and while they were dining. Mr and Mrs Love did not wish to see the crew sunbathing. White uniforms would be provided, worn at all times and kept spotless. When Mr and Mrs Love entertained on board there were three cardinal rules for the entire crew to observe: the guest is always right; the answer is always 'yes'; no sitting down where a guest can see you.

Now the bastard crew had bailed out, and she was going to have to spend hours writing it all out again. But it was the only way. That cruise last year on the Kilmartin's yacht had been a five-star screw-up. Their table manners! Heck, you'd think these aristos would *know* that you never eat chicken bones with your fingers. Lamb or beef, yes. Poultry, no.

Joleen drew towards her a sheaf of headed writing paper her, was by far a classier choice than gold.

Still, things weren't looking so hunky-dory for the Dockers these days. Lady Kilmartin had telephoned Joleen with the news that since Sir Bernard had been ousted from Daimler the Dockers had been forced to sell Norah's jewellery, and now they were tax exiles on Jersey.

'They're living in a bungalow!' Lady Kilmartin's laugh rang down the line like gunshot. 'Poor Norah. She says the people on Jersey are the most frightfully boring, dreadful people that have ever been born.'

Lady Docker living in a bungalow! I won't tell Colin, Joleen decided. We must be seen to stack up with success. And at least the Dockers have still got the yacht.

'Are you crazy? I told you a month ago, a Mediterranean cruise is not affordable. The boat is not affordable.' Ronald C. Beck shoved the yacht accounts across his desk at Colin. 'Quite apart from the fuel, just look how much the crew costs.'

'I don't get it,' Colin said. 'I paid them top dollar. And now they've scarpered.'

Ronald C. Beck brightened. 'So the trip's off?'

Colin shook his head. 'Some chance. Joleen's trying to fix a Med meet with Sir Bernard and Lady Docker.'

'Christ. They the dudes with the silver-plated Rolls-Royce?'

'Daimler. Joleen is slavering. What I haven't told her is that the Docker dame had a run-in with Prince Rainier. She completely lost her temper and threw the Monaco flag on the floor. So now Rainier's managed to have her banned from the entire Côte d'Azur.'

His accountant took off his jacket. Pulled up a chair next to his client. 'Now listen up, Colin. You have got to get into your head that you're in deep financial shit. Deep. We've talked about it. I told you, when you started the company you were ahead of the pack in the "fast food" business. But now there's others coming up on the rails. They're more streamlined than you, more cost-efficient.'

Colin was staring out of the window.

'The boat, Colin, has got to go. And the London house.'

'I can't tell her yet, Ronnie. She's in thick with Lady This and Lord That in Mayfair. And having the boat, London, Manhattan, moving in those sort of circles, it all means so much to her, after the way she grew up.'

'Bottom line, Colin,' said Ronald. 'You need to raise a million.'

Colin whistled. 'A million dollars . . .'

'Pounds. I always figure your accounts in pounds, like you asked me to. You gotta sell the boat, sell London, stop being so generous to your staff and . . .'

No need for Ronnie to say it. They both knew the kill line: 'Stop being so indulgent to your wife.'

At last Colin got his walk in Central Park. He was on his way to meet Ilona's hotshot lawyer for lunch. Patric Ryan.

Lunch was his shout. Never met him before. What did he want?

He took deep breaths in the bright-blue New York sunshine. He treasured the park. Who would have thought skyscrapers could look so sexy? It was all so blissfully far, far from the Isle of Wight.

Colin was born there, above his parents' workmen's caff. When his father went away to war, his mother took over the place, and it became a working women's enclave, as the girls took the men's jobs in the factories.

After school Colin helped his mum. He loved it. He was a great favourite with the factory girls and Ilona's gang. They used to drop in after school, ravenous for toast. Colin couldn't understand it. Ilona's parents were stinking rich, so at her house there would have been not just toast but jam and cake for tea. Yet she and Paula preferred to hang out at the caff. Weird.

Then the war ended, and it all changed. The men came back. Soft voices and the tap of high heels were drowned by the clomp of boots, gruff hilarity and barked commands. The women changed; got all soppy and laughed in a trilly way. Colin was no longer encouraged to be the women's pet. Aged sixteen, his father sent him to work as an apprentice printer.

More men. Tough, demanding, shrewd. Colin could have tolerated the robust atmosphere, but what he couldn't do, and what with hot-metal type it was essential that he could do, was read the type in mirror-image. He found it impossible. All the letters went into a blur.

After a month he arrived back at the caff at four thirty in the afternoon. Early. His mother was drying teacups. His father was standing by the stove, frying eggs and smoking his pipe.

'What's up, son?' said his mother. 'You ill?'

'No.' Colin still remembered it as one of the worst

moments of his life. 'I, well, I've been asked to leave.'

His mother went white. 'Oh dear!'

His father banged the frying pan into the sink. 'Fired! You bin fired! You had a job for life and, you stupid twerp, you bin fired!'

The entire caff went silent. They knew what was coming. They'd heard it all before, tactfully leaving Colin alone when he went down the alley afterwards and cried.

Colin could see Ilona and Paula and the back of a girl he didn't know with mad tawny hair. They were sharing a plateful of toast. With all his heart he wished he could be sitting with them, ribbing the girls about their Guides badges.

'Right,' bellowed his father. 'Yard. NOW!'

The yard was at the back of the shop. At the bottom was a privy containing a chemical toilet shared by three other families. There was constant dispute about whose turn it was to clean it out. Next to the privy was a wooden bench. When Mr Love had come back from the war he had made the bench. Colin had heard him telling his mother that the boy needed toughening up.

Toughening up Colin involved two activities in the yard. Sometimes Mr Love, wearing his heavy black boots, would give his son what was known as a good kicking. Today Colin's father appeared in the yard with a leather belt in his hand. 'Right. Get across it.'

As Colin bent over the bench and the thrashing began, the thought that penetrated through the pain was that they could all hear. Everyone in the caff. All his mates. And the families who shared the lavatory, they could all see. The shame of it! Just don't let me cry, Colin pleaded with himself. Not yet.

He had his eye on the back gate because usually what he did afterwards was go down the alley and blub where no one could see him. He saw the gate burst open.

Suddenly the yard was inhabited by a wild animal. 'Leave him alone, you goddamn bully!'

With difficulty Colin straightened up, astounded that someone so skinny could make so much noise. (He was used to it now, of course.) He stared at her. She had tawny hair and yellow eyes. Good grief, she had yellow eyes.

Colin's father, army trained, recovered fast and advanced on the girl. 'And just who are you, missy? I'll teach you –'

She did what Colin had always dreamed of doing but never dared. She smiled a dazzling smile at Mr Love, snatched the leather belt and whacked him a stinging blow across the face.

As Mr Love howled in pain, the girl flicked her thumb towards the gate. 'Come on, Colin.'

He never went home again.

Joleen. He'd never heard the name before. As they escaped down the road to get the bus to her uncle's house, she told him he was an ex-GI who had married an English girl – 'and don't worry, if your pa comes calling my uncle will pulverize him'.

She'd been on the Isle of Wight a month and got friendly with Ilona and the gang at the caff. 'That's how I knew your name and how to say it. *Coll*in. Where I come from in the States we say it *Coal*in. *Coll*in is nicer. I like things to be nice.'

'Why were the girls talking about me?' asked Colin as they clambered to the top of the bus.

Joleen giggled. 'Because they told me they both used to be sweet on you.'

She saw his look of amazement and regarded him fondly. Dark wavy hair, liquid brown eyes, generous mouth. My, he was cute. And he had no idea what he'd got.

Colin was thinking, Hang on, I live over a caff. Girls like Ilona and Paula – way out of reach.

'You said they used to, you know, be keen on me?'

Joleen handed tuppence to the clippie. 'Well, you know how it is. Someone else came along.'

Colin frowned. 'No. You've got that wrong. I've never seen Ilona or Paula with a boy.'

Joleen laughed.

A year later he heard that Ilona had eloped. With a German. Bloody hell.

By that time Joleen and Colin were living in the States. They worked their passage on a mail ship, and Joleen's uncle lent them the money to open their own coffee-shop.

They called it Lovebites. Joleen's idea. It was an instant success, and they paid off the uncle's loan within six months. Soon they had a chain of Lovebites. It was hard work, fourteen hours a day, seven days a week, but it was worth it. And it was fun.

Joleen was such a wacky, wonderful girl in those days, thought Colin, completing his peaceful stroll in Central Park. She had ideas, she worked her butt off, she was sexy as hell. If it wasn't for Joleen, I'd have nothing, he admitted to himself.

And he heard the voice of Ronald C. Beck reminding him: If it wasn't for her you wouldn't be up the Swannee to the tune of a million quid.

A million! Oh God, oh shit.

SEVEN

'FANCY THE WHIP, Kit?'

Hiding her laughter at the lust in her lover's eyes, Liz linked arms with Ilona as they skirted the coconut shy.

'A fair? A real English fair? What fun!' Liz had enthused, thinking what hell, what absolute hell.

Kit had driven them to Cimiez, a fashionable neighbourhood overlooking Nice, and Paula had immediately made a bee-line for the dodgems. She was still there, furiously bashing into everyone and complaining that her car wouldn't go fast enough.

'Scares the life out of me,' Liz said, wincing at the flashing lights and blaring music of the Whip. 'You take Ilona up, Kit.'

She urged them into the Whip car, pulled down the iron bar to hold them in, then leaned against the candy-floss tent for a fag and a rest. Ilona and Kit waved. Grinning, Liz waved back. Ilona held up the bear Kit had won for her at the shooting gallery. She waved its arm. Beaming, Liz waved at the bear.

God, she hated fairs. The gagging smell of diesel, frankfurters and onions. The fairground men with their weasel faces and greasy hair. The brutal lights, senseless music, the screams.

But for the past two hours Liz had swept Ilona and Kit round the rides and stalls in a blaze of vivacity and calculated nostalgia. Capitalizing on the many years that had passed since Ilona had been to an English fairground, Liz exclaimed over the coconuts and figurines of china ladies playing the organ, 'Just the same tasteless prizes, Ilona. Some things never change.'

Her dilemma had been how to soften Ilona up and get her and Kit on physical terms without the aid of alcohol. The fair had seemed the ideal solution. Lots of kidding around, casual touching and Kit's manly arm to protect Ilona on the scary rides. Stubbing out her cigarette, she watched the white-faced pair whirling round in the Whip and willed Kit not to be sick.

She checked her watch. If she was at home she would be getting back from work now, shoving Kit into the kitchen while she sat down to listen to *The Archers*. Yet here they were on the French Riviera trying to pull off a con trick that was, let's face it, as fragile as a party paperchain.

The Whip was slowing down. Liz adjusted her expression and put on the crocodile hat made of turquoise foam that was her booby-prize when she'd lost at the shooting gallery. Smiling broadly, she strolled towards the ride. It was Ilona's and Kit's turn to get off. Kit helped Ilona to her feet, waved to Liz and swung back the iron bar. Ilona descended from the ride. Liz took one look at her and broke into a run.

'There's been an incident,' Paula reported later to Patric. 'We were at the fair. Ilona came off one of those whirly-round things and passed out.'

'Hurt herself?'

'No, thanks to Kit. She said she felt faint. I always thought people fainted backwards. But Kit knew to get in *front* of her, and he caught her. I wondered how he knew that, but Liz remembered that he had done a couple of years at medical school. Anyway he drove us very smoothly home, and Ilona's absolutely fine.'

'I'm glad you call it home.'

'Actually I think she's got an aversion to sugar. She had some candy floss.'

'What have you got on?'

'What have *you* got on?'

'Coleman Hawkins. "Body and Soul". Talking of which –'

'All right. A sarong and a red swimsuit. I'm going for a midnight dip.'

'One day I want to see you swim naked.'

'Ilona swims naked every morning, early.'

'What, in full view of all of you? Has that chap Kit seen her?'

'Don't know. Probably not. He's usually last down to breakfast.'

'I shall never be able to do it, Lizzie.'

'Nonsense. She's got a great body.' Liz had dragged him to her window this morning to peek as Ilona dived into the pool. 'She had her own gym and pool at the Schloss.'

Kit reached for her. 'I prefer you. I only ever want you, Lizzie.'

'Here she comes,' announced Kit, binoculars trained on the *Lovebite II* as she sailed into Cannes. One hundred and thirty feet, dark-blue hull, white raked funnel, elegant line. She was flying three flags from the foremast: the Bahamian (she was registered in Nassau), the Stars and

Stripes and, beneath these, the courtesy flag, the French *Tricolore*.

Joleen had telephoned from Antibes to say they would not be dining on board as the catering crew were too new to be relied on. She and Colin looked forward to welcoming them aboard for cocktails at six thirty, and he had booked two cars to take them to dinner afterwards.

'Where?' asked Paula.

Ilona shrugged. 'She just said that place up the hill.'

'Oh, for heaven's sake!' Paula was exasperated. 'If there's one thing that annoys me it's people who don't know which restaurant they're going to and when they get back they haven't a clue where they've been.'

Liz went off to get changed. For once she totally agreed with Paula. You'd have thought, having been in the catering business, Joleen would take a professional interest in where they were eating and why.

Brushing her hair, Liz's hand was shaking. She chose a daisy-printed dress so if her hands got clammy she could discreetly wipe them on the skirt. This Joleen sounded sharp as a knife, and Liz had been unable to get any dirt on her. Every time Liz had ventured a question Paula and Ilona exchanged glances and said vaguely, 'Oh, she and Colin are old, old friends. They're so looking forward to meeting Kit – and you, too, of course, Lizzie.'

Red-faced, Liz tugged angrily at her zip. Will she find us out?

The sun had not yet set, and they agreed to walk the short distance to the harbour.

Paula had been mugging up on Cannes so appointed herself tour guide. 'We'll soon be passing the Villa Eleanor. Built by Lord Brougham in memory of his daughter. Lord Brougham was the Lord Chancellor of England. He was trying to get to Italy for the winter, but there was a cholera epidemic in Nice, so he stayed in this little fishing village, loved it and made it fashionable. Queen Victoria came, as well as loads of English aristos, and lots of them built villas. So the Villa Eleanor was Lord Brougham's main residence, but a few doors away he built another house, Carpe Diem. Seize the day.'

This last was helpfully directed at Liz who felt like throttling her. I did Latin at school, thank you.

Paula sailed on, 'Carpe Diem was built to house his lordship's mistresses . . .'

Liz felt hot. So hot she felt like a bundle of boiled puddings.

The afternoon had been frightful. Ilona had returned from the local shop with the intelligence that on the outskirts of Cannes there was an excellent hairdresser who spoke English. Liz rang to make an appointment for Ilona and to ask for directions.

'Oh, eet is easy. You go past ze train station, and ze road she bend, and you see Valérie Coiffeur in front.'

It was a boiling-hot afternoon, and they hit a traffic jam coming into Cannes. Liz, hatless, was cooking behind the wheel of Patric's white convertible. At last they passed the station, rounded a bend, came out of Cannes and there was no sign of Valérie Coiffeur.

'It's not there, Liz,' confirmed Ilona, ravishing in a cream straw sunhat tied with a pale-blue silk scarf. 'You'll have to telephone them.'

Liz parked in the shade. The phone box felt like it was already running with sweat.

'Eet is easy,' insisted Valérie. 'We are next to ze 'otel.'

'Which hotel?'

'Ze one wiz ze red shutters.'

'What's it called?'

'Eet does not 'ave a name.'

'All hotels have a name.'

'Of course. Eet 'ave a name – ze Hôtel Zizi. But now ze 'otel ees shut.'

Liz shoved more francs into the slot. 'Right. Just tell me your exact address.'

'I do not know eet.'

'You must know your own address!'

'*Non*. Ze *mairie*, they 'ave changed all ze streets and all ze numbers. No one ees 'appy. You come to ze house with ze red shutters, and in front you see three dustbins painted red. We are next door. You find us. Eet –'

'I know,' sighed Liz. 'It's easy.'

Amazingly, it was easy. 'There must have been a lorry blocking our sightline,' said Ilona. She stepped from the car and took from the back seat a daintily flowered hat box. She smiled at Liz's evident confusion. 'I want to wear a cocktail hat tonight, but I'm hopeless at getting it to sit right. I thought Valérie could sort of arrange my hair round it.'

Marvellous, thought Liz. I get sunstroke driving you to a hairdresser so you can have a hat stuck on.

'Aren't you having your hair done, Lizzie?'

'No. I loathe hairdressers,' lied Liz.

Someone who could afford a hairdresser – or thought she could – was Joleen. But today she'd been obliged to create her bouffant herself. Unthinkable, of course, to trust any hairdresser in Antibes. It was the one big drawback to having a boat. You had to do your hair yourself, your nails yourself and get your dress on yourself. Next trip out she really was going to bring her maid.

With her hair sprayed into place she ran a cool bath, revelling in the soothing water. Lady Kilmartin's boat had no baths, just godawful showers that trickled, Lady Docker said.

'How's it going?' Colin banged on the door.

Why did he do that? Ask how's it going when he meant how much longer are you going to be?

'Use one of the others, Col.'

'You told me not to. You said I'd mess it up for the guests.'

'Well, use it anyway and get a stewardess to mop up after you.'

At six o'clock she went up to the afterdeck to supervise the steward laying out the food. Joleen was wearing a sugar-pink satin dress with a bell skirt, accessorized with a gold necklace, gold earrings and five gold bracelets. She pointed a talon at a salver of something she did not recognize.

'What's that?' You never knew with a Norwegian chef. She certainly didn't want plates of stuff with names that had no meaning. Smorge and sild. What the heck were they about?

'It's minced chicken with pineapple, on blinis, madam,' said the senior steward.

'What's a blini?'

'A cracker tends to go soggy under a topping, but a blini is soft but firm so holds the topping neatly.'

'Soft but firm,' repeated Joleen. OK. She checked the flowers. She checked that the champagne was chilled and that someone had cleaned up after Colin. At six twenty-five she called, 'Places, everyone', and took up her position by the silver rose bowl in the salon.

Arriving at the *Lovebite II* moored alongside most of the new Cannes harbour wall, Liz had to force herself not to gawp. She had always, always wanted to go on a yacht, and, oh boy, was this some yacht. The motor-yacht looked massive, dominating all the other boats in the harbour, her hull painted classy dark blue, with the name picked out in white.

The crisply dressed steward on the harbour-side assisted Ilona towards the gangway, and when she reached the top, guiding herself carefully with the single rope rail, she was greeted by a stiff salute from the blond Norwegian skipper and a welcoming kiss from Colin.

Paula followed. Then Liz. Or, rather, not Liz. The gangway crossed two feet of open water. She stared at the gap with rising horror.

'What's up, Lizzie?' whispered Kit.

'I can't do it, Kit. I can't cross this bridge thing. I'll fall in.'

'You won't. Just grab the rope rail.'

'It's moving. That rail's moving.'

'Yes, well, it's rope.'

'I can't, Kit!' Her voice rose. 'I'll fall in!' She burst into tears and flung herself at him.

Somehow Kit managed to stay in character. Couldn't do anything else, he told her later, with Colin, Ilona and Paula staring wide-eyed at the whole sorry performance. 'Here, steady on, Lizzie.' He detached her from him, patted her shoulder. 'There, there.'

On deck Captain Knut addressed Colin. 'Permission to assist the lady aboard, sir.'

'Carry on, skipper,' Colin said smartly.

Drying her eyes on Kit's handkerchief, Liz saw an enormous man hurtling down the gangway. He was huge. Now he was on the quay looming over her. Now he was – oh God! Knut had picked her up, thrown her over his shoulder and was carrying her aboard.

Needless to say, she was scarlet as she shook hands with Colin.

'Damn stupid, that rickety gangway,' Colin told her. 'I'll get something done about it. Now come and meet Joleen. I know she's dying to show you round the boat.'

Unaware of the drama, his wife was waiting by the rose bowl surveying with satisfaction the décor of the salon. The carpet swirled in gold and lemon, the wallpaper on the port side featured bamboo leaves, and on the starboard side an amusing design of cocktail glasses and maraschino cherries led the eye to the high-stooled bar.

The sofas were covered in maroon moquette, grouped round circular prong-legged occasional tables topped with mosaics depicting fish and sea urchins. The salon, considered Joleen, was perfect. When she got back to Manhattan she'd replicate the look there.

As Ilona, Paula and Joleen fell into huggy reunion mode, Liz gazed at her surroundings with disbelief. OK, she knew bright colours and four different sorts of wallpaper in one room were all the rage, but this was an Italian-designed boat. It cried out for elegance, not décor that gave you a headache.

Joleen swept them through a dining-room that could seat twelve and invited them to see her bedroom, which she referred to as the stateroom.

The stateroom was a hymn to mauve. The walls were mauve, splashed with purple. The curtains glowed deep plum. There was a lilac satin bedspread, edged with gold and topped with lavender silk cushions adorned with prune tassels.

Liz observed Kit trying to keep a straight face.

'And this!' Joleen burst out triumphantly, patting a contraption on her bedside table. 'Bet you can't guess what this is.'

They all gazed at the device, and Paula pronounced, 'It's a Teasmade.'

'Oh,' wailed Joleen. 'You weren't supposed to know.'

'Well, it's my job to keep up with new catering stuff. And trust you to have the very latest!'

Mollified, Joleen ushered them up to the afterdeck for champagne.

'Just water for me, thanks,' requested Ilona.

'And me,' said Liz.

Joleen signalled to the steward, who signalled to a junior

crew member stationed outside the galley. 'We have iced water, naturally. Well, I say naturally. You'd be surprised the people who don't. The Kilmartins' water wasn't just tepid; it tasted filthy. I said to Colin, didn't I, Col . . .'

As Joleen went on Liz felt increasingly queasy. Sitting up here was like sitting on the roof of a three-storey house, awaiting rescue from floodwater all around.

There was a fantastic view, of course, across the glistening harbour and up to the ancient old town of Le Suquet. But Liz would have appreciated it more if only the *Lovebite* would stop moving. She hadn't realized that even when tethered a boat can still move. As it swayed almost imperceptibly to and fro, to and fro, Liz's stomach started to sway, too.

'Do have a blini,' offered Joleen. 'They're specially made to be soft but firm. And the topping is minced chicken with pineapple and cream –'

'I'm terribly sorry,' Liz said urgently. 'I don't feel well.'

'Oh, you poor thing.' Joleen was instantly all hostessy concern. 'Come and lie down on my bed.'

The prospect of lying in a room that reminded her of rhubarb crumble finished it for Liz.

'If you don't mind, I think I'll go back to the villa.'

'I'll call the car for you,' said Joleen.

'No I'd rather walk, thanks. Clear my head.'

Kit stood up. 'I'll come with you.'

'No,' said Colin. 'I'll take her.'

As soon as Joleen saw Colin and Liz disappear down the quay, she exploded. 'What a godawful dress. Cotton! Do you think she made it herself?'

'At least you can wash cotton,' said Ilona. 'Your dry-cleaning bills must be enormous.'

Joleen nodded happily. 'Thank God I'm not poor.'

Kit took his champagne over to the rail, his eyes raking the harbour for Lizzie and Colin. Where the hell were they? Colin seemed a decent enough bloke, and, God knows, he had enough to put up with, with that viper of a wife. But what was he up to with Lizzie? Where were they?

They were in a bar. Colin was ordering Liz a cognac to settle her stomach. Getting off the *Lovebite* had proved just as tricky for Liz as getting on, but at least she hadn't had to involve Knut. And, oh, the relief of being on dry land!

'What's so stupid about me being stupid on your boat, Colin, is that I've always wanted to go on a boat like yours.'

She told him about the *Lady Jenny*, her yearning for it and the screams of laughter from her schoolmates.

Sipping her cognac she went on, 'The funny thing is, I'm fine on a cross-Channel ferry.'

'There's boats and boats,' Colin said, as they left the bar.

Liz said, 'I'll be fine if you want to get back. Joleen –'

'Knows I'm seeing you home.'

Colin took her arm as they crossed the road. They walked in silence for a bit, and then he said abruptly, 'Joleen. She – I mean, I know what you must think.'

Liz busied herself blowing her nose.

'But the thing is, if you could have seen Joleen when we first went into business. She was bright as a button, worked like a slave – and did we laugh! I remember, after we started the business in America, we thought we'd have a crack at England. Our first caff there was on the Great North Road. We were driving back to London late that night with the takings. We had fish and chips and a car full of cash, and we stopped in a layby and . . . oh, she was fantastic.'

They strolled past gardens scented with jasmine and roses, and Liz said, 'Funny how sometimes you long for something and then, when you get it, it just isn't what you hoped for.'

'Yeah. It's just . . . it was all so much simpler then. And you think, can you ever get that back?'

Liz smiled but said nothing as they approached the villa.

He followed her into the hall and gazed appreciatively in on the salon, taking in the Aubusson carpet, the imposing marble fireplace, the champagne-coloured silk curtains and the Bösendorfer grand. It was all so restful. He'd have liked to stretch out on one of the deep sofas and listen to some music. Classical. Not the jumpy stuff Joleen went for.

Joleen. This bloody dinner at this poncey restaurant. Why couldn't they have had something simple on the boat? On the piano he spotted the silver-framed wedding photo of Ilona and Hans. He picked it up. 'Ah, yes. We all got one of these. Handsome chap, wasn't he?'

Liz accompanied him to the big main gates. 'I saw some mint growing near the path. I'm going to tuck myself in bed with some nice mint tea.'

As Colin walked away he looked back at her picking mint and thought, What a decent woman. Really sympathetic. Doesn't talk all the time. Doesn't argue. Really, really nice.

Liz dumped the mint on the kitchen table and opened the cupboard where Constanza kept spare keys to all the rooms. Ilona, interestingly, with all her jewels and precious bits of silver, never locked her bedroom door. Paula always did.

So what, wondered Liz, did she have to hide? With Constanza keeping a gimlet eye on the household, Liz had never before dared break into Paula's room. But tonight, with everyone out and Constanza off duty, this was her chance.

She hurried upstairs, shoved the key in the lock, and

then she was in. Calm room, solid wood furniture, huge double bed. She thought of her and Kit crushed into her single and sighed.

Forced herself to concentrate. Bedside cabinet. Nothing unusual. Wardrobe. She riffled through all the shelves, then looked in Paula's shoes. Nothing.

The walnut bureau. Please don't let the bitch have locked it. Please let the key be lost.

It opened. The top pulled down, and in the cavity at the back sat a loose-leaf folder. Liz took it to the bed. She was hoping it was a diary, but it proved to be a record of another kind: Provençal recipes that Paula had been collecting for her book.

Impatiently, Liz flicked through to the end. She found a crappy poem. And photos! This was more like it. Here was Paula and a thick-set guy, smiley, happy, obviously on holiday. And then another photo. A man. Tall, blond, elegant. A gardenia in his buttonhole.

Smiling in triumph, Liz studied the picture, although she didn't really need to, as she had seen the man every day on the rosewood grand piano in the salon. Her smile softened. 'You're right, Col. He was a handsome devil.'

EIGHT

Two Mercedes were waiting on the harbour to ferry the party to the restaurant.

Joleen, anxious to catch up on the news with her old girl-friends and, as usual, livid with Colin, wanted a girl car and a boy car. Kit, however, conscious of his future dreaded responsibilities, steered Ilona to the first car, slid on to the leather seat beside her and slammed the door.

In car two the conversation on the pretty drive into the wooded hills was decidedly edgy.

Joleen poked Colin in the back. 'Why were you so *long*?'

'I had to take Liz home.'

'Crap. There were lots of people about. She'd have been home safe in no time.'

'She wasn't well. When I left she was picking mint. For tea. To settle her stomach.'

Joleen sat back in her seat and smoothed her satin skirt. 'Hey, I'm glad she's not here. That dress! I'm sure she made it herself.'

'Actually she did,' said Paula. 'She told me. I think it's clever if you can make your own clothes.'

'I tell you, I was raised having to make mine, and I'm

74

damned glad I don't have to any more. When Col and I first got married I used to make his shirts. Didn't I, Col?'

'I'm sure you still could,' he said, thinking: A million quid! We're a million in the red.

Joleen hooted.

Their destination was the Moulin d'Or, one of the most celebrated restaurants in all France. It started as a farmhouse *auberge* much favoured by local artists who came in the evenings, particularly in winter, to relax by the wood fire and eat peasant Provençal food very cheaply. When even cheap was unaffordable they paid the bill by leaving a painting. Picasso did it, as did Chagall and Klein.

Eventually the *auberge* expanded into a full-blown restaurant, and, because of the fabulous cuisine and what had become valuable works of art on the wall, the Moulin d'Or established its reputation as the place in which to be seen.

Joleen, Colin realized with a sinking heart, was certainly determined to be seen. The woman in sugar-pink greeted the manager like an old friend, name-dropped maître d's and restaurants she knew in New York, and finally they were all shown to a table in the garden where they were visible to all.

The garden was glorious, candlelit, with white flowers glowing in the falling light, their luminescence enhanced by columns of mirrors. Heavens, thought Paula, with the torrential rain they get here from time to time how do they keep all that glass clean?

When the champagne had arrived and Joleen was interrogating the waiter about the provenance of the prawns, Ilona murmured to Colin, 'Isn't that Viscount Nuffield just coming in? He came to lunch at the Schloss once.'

Colin gulped. Lord Nuffield. Morris cars. Worth at least £75 million. And all I need is one! Just one measly million. Christ, it wasn't fair.

He croaked hopefully to Ilona, 'Are you going to say hello?'

'Oh no. He spent most of the time closeted with Hans. Talking business, I suppose. He wouldn't remember me.'

Kit was just about to claim her attention with a smooth if obvious compliment when he felt sugar-pink talons closing round the arm of his jacket.

'So. Kit. Tell me about yourself.'

Oh God, thought Kit. Liz, Lizzie darling, where are you? He smiled his easy smile. 'I grew up in the country –'

'The second son of Earl Rowledge,' chipped in Paula, just to watch Joleen have a public orgasm.

'I went to boarding-school. Did well at sport, mainly.' And fighting. It was that sort of expensive school. 'Then there was the Navy for my National Service, and after that my father wanted me to do medicine. But it wasn't for me. I left after a couple of years and went to sea. Crewing. Then I got my own boat and ran a charter business.'

'What was it called?' asked Joleen.

'What?'

'Your boat. What was it called.'

'Oh.' Mayday, mayday. He wished he'd never gone down this route. No one forgot the name of their boat, did they?

'Er, *Audrey*,' he told them. 'It – it was my mother's name.'

Joleen wasn't letting go. 'Was it *The Audrey*?'

'No. Just *Audrey*.'

'Not *Audrey II*?'

'No.'

'He's just told you,' cut in Colin. 'It's just *Audrey*.'

'Ours is *Lovebite II*,' Joleen told Kit.

Colin shuddered at the memory of *Lovebite I*; eggyolk-yellow hull and an interior featuring what seemed like miles of Joleen's favourite fabric of the time, fake leopard.

'And how did you meet Liz?'

Liz had rehearsed Kit thoroughly on this one, so the lies

flowed fluently. While he was on National Service Liz came as secretary to his father, and Kit got to know her, just briefly, on his leaves. Such a jolly girl!

'What did your parents say when you dropped out of medical school?' asked Ilona.

'Well, my mother died when I was young, and then my father went midway through my time as a medic, so I was free, really, to suit myself.'

Colin watched his wife put on her motherly you-can-confide-in-me face as she squeezed Kit's arm, crooning, 'And what about girlfriends, Kit? Is there anyone special?'

Colin felt for the guy. But there was nothing he could do, not with the girls all agog.

Kit took a casual sip of wine. He was on red alert. He and Lizzie had discussed this one endlessly.

'We can't say that there was someone but she left you. Ilona might think you're a lousy lover.'

'Probably will be. You know I can only do it with you.'

'Rubbish. Just get on top and think of the money. Anyway, we don't want Ilona thinking you're carrying a torch for someone else. On the other hand, we don't want you looking unpopular.'

'Or queer.'

Finally, what they came up with was what Kit was now, with quiet sincerity, telling Joleen. 'Of course there were girls. But being at sea so much there wasn't time to develop a settled relationship.'

Paula leaned forward. 'So you'd like to settle down?'

Kit looked directly at Ilona. 'Yes I would. Very much.'

'Colin, I'm sure that's Lady Comyn over there,' said Joleen. 'Do go and remind her who we are.'

'I am not speaking to that stuck-up cow. I'm going to the gents'.'

On his way back Colin was passing through the bar when he spotted a Bogart look-alike lounging underneath a painting by Picasso. It was Skip, who had been nominally in charge of Colin's first boat.

Skip was grinning at him. 'Hallo, cock.'

Colin recognized long ago that he had never managed to establish the ideal master–servant relationship with his ex-skipper. 'What are you doing here, Skip?' Meaning, I wouldn't have thought you could afford the Moulin d'Or.

'Driving Lady Comyn.' Skip relit his roll-up. 'But you should have seen the last job I had. Arabian prince. Had a collection of Rollers. Took a different one out every day, brum-brum down the Croisette. But he never learned how to park any of them. So I'd follow behind so I could leap out and park the Roller for him. Anyway,' he stubbed out his fag, 'I got my own boat now, Col. *Skip's Tub*, she's called. You should come and see. Moored at Antibes.'

They chatted on, talking boats. Colin was in no hurry to return to his party, and for all his scurrilous ways Skip was always entertaining company.

'Where have you been, Colin?' snapped Joleen as he reluctantly rejoined the table.

'Remember Skip?'

Joleen made a face.

'He's in the bar. Doing all right. Got his own boat now.'

Patting himself on the back for avoiding any mention of Skip's chauffeuring for Lady Comyn, Colin realized almost immediately that he'd shot himself in the foot, because Joleen was launching relentlessly into the donkey story.

'We were moored off Greece, and Colin had given the crew shore leave for the evening. They got plastered, of course, and I blame Skip for that, I really do. Anyway they came back in the tender, and in it was a donkey.'

'Alive?' said Paula.

'Oh yes. The owner had been beating S-H-I-T out of it on the beach, so Skip bought it off him, and then they didn't know what to do with it, so they thought, hey, ships have cats so why not a ship's donkey?'

'So what did you do, Colin?' Kit was enjoying himself. At least the heat was off him for a bit.

'Gave the crew a bollocking – excuse me, girls – and then, well, let's face it, a donkey is hardly a seafaring animal, is it?'

Joleen was shrieking with laughter. 'He took it back! Col took the donkey back.'

'I felt sorry for it. I wanted to find a better owner.'

Joleen squeezed his hand. 'I know. It just shows you're a very nice man, Col.'

'Yes, well, the Greek police didn't think so. I'd just got the sopping animal ashore when two Greek rozzers rushed up and arrested me.'

'What for?' asked Ilona.

'Illegally importing an animal. They chucked me in the slammer. Didn't believe me when I said I owned the *Lovebite*.'

'What Colin's forgotten to tell you,' choked Joleen, 'is that all he was wearing was pyjamas. He had no money, passport, documents, anything.'

In the end Colin had managed to persuade the Greek police to go to the boat and check.

'I was fast asleep,' said Joleen. 'I knew nothing of any of this. Suddenly there's this Greek cop on deck ranting on about my husband and a donkey. I thought he was crazy. Then Skip came lurching up and explained.' She turned to Ilona. 'The thing was, I was wearing that pink nightie. The one you sent me from Paris.'

'I remember,' smiled Ilona. 'That Greek cop must have got quite an eyeful.'

'An eyeful and an earful,' said Joleen. 'I went berserk. Insisted he take me ashore, and, of course, I immediately sprang Colin from the cooler.'

Colin wished she'd stop telling the donkey story. It always made him feel such a prat.

Then, to his horror, he saw that Joleen was signalling to the waiter for more champagne. It was another thing he wished she wouldn't do. He was the bloke. It wasn't her place to order booze. And champagne! Hadn't they had enough?

'None for me,' demurred Ilona.

'Nor me, thanks,' said Kit. Liz had insisted he cut back when he was with Ilona. 'Don't worry, I'll keep a bottle in my room for us to share. But you'll have to make sure you clean your teeth before you go downstairs.'

Paula had her hand over her glass. 'I don't –'

'Oh, come on,' Joleen said briskly. 'This dinner's our treat, isn't it, Colin?'

Colin felt himself going white inside. Words like *arm* and *leg* and *prison* stabbed at him.

Paula said, 'No, no, Joleen, we can't have that. It's traditional, isn't it, that when the owners leave the boat the guests pay for dinner.'

Now it was Kit feeling nauseous. It was as if he could see his wallet, empty, forlorn, floating away.

'Sure, that's good of you,' said Joleen. 'You know, normally I would have entertained you all on the yacht. But we have a new crew,' she glared at Colin, ' and I haven't had time to train them yet. You know, the other day a steward brought Colin a gin and tonic, with ice, of course, and there was so much condensation on the glass Colin got it all down the front of his shorts. What did he look like? I said to the steward, I said how could you be so stupid, don't you know you always bring a serviette?'

Fortunately, while Paula was restraining herself from pointing out that the English word was napkin, not serviette, the singing started. They were a group of unaccompanied singers who simply stood underneath a linden tree and sang. Songs you could sway to: 'By the Light of the Silvery

Moon', 'Give My Regards to Broadway', 'When Irish Eyes Are Smiling'.

'Don't you just love a cappella?' Ilona murmured to Kit.

He smiled, baffled, wondering if a cappella was an Italian dessert.

Luckily she went on, 'In fact, any music out of doors is special, don't you think?'

Kit, who had no musical ear whatsoever, held her lovely eyes with his and breathed, 'Absolutely. Unforgettable.'

The performance ended. Through the applause Paula watched Ilona looking at Kit's mouth as he lit an Olivier.

Joleen shot to her feet. 'Wow! How brilliant was that! We must invite them to our party.'

Colin grabbed her wrist. 'Hold on. What party?'

'I wanted to have it on the boat, Col. You know it looks so pretty all lit up. But then I wanted to invite Lady Comyn and Lady Kilmartin, and I thought of that goddamn crew and –'

'So we're having it at the villa,' Ilona told him. 'It'll be fun. Our group will all wear dresses the colours of the rainbow. Mine's red. I've always wanted to be a scarlet woman.'

Joleen snatched back her wrist from her husband and raced off to nobble star guests for the party. Colin excused himself to pay the bill. Kit followed. Paula watched Ilona watching Kit all the way through the garden.

Colin was at the desk counting out an Everest of francs.

'Let me chip in on this,' Kit offered.

'Good of you. Thanks. But no need.'

'At least let me buy you a stiff drink.'

Colin decided this Kit was all right. He'd not been sure at first.

When at last they got back Joleen was too busy table-hopping to have noticed Colin's absence. Colin prayed Ilona wouldn't mention Lord Nuffield. So far Joleen hadn't recognized him. And there was an unspoken agreement among them all not to mention that Winston Churchill was in the south of France, on the Onassis yacht.

As he slid into his seat Paula heard Ilona say quietly to Kit, 'If you don't mind me saying so, you have a very elegant walk. Wonderful posture.'

'Oh, the Navy did that for me. Before that I was just a public-school layabout.'

Colin said to Paula, 'You look very thoughtful. Penny for them?'

She said slowly, 'I was wondering . . . I was wondering what happened to the donkey.'

'You offered to do *what*?' Liz whispered loudly and furiously. '*What!*'

It was later that night. Kit, naked in her bed, was trying to get the cork out of a bottle of rosé – silently. Not easy but he managed it.

'Look, Paula had already offered to do the food for the party, so I thought the least I could do was volunteer to run the bar.'

'You bloody fool. For a start, we don't want any questions about where you learned bar-tending skills.' Her mind ricocheted back to Le Touquet, the casino bar where she'd found Kit raiding the till.

'It's OK. Ilona stepped in. She's insisting on getting in caterers. I gather you and Paula have got to oversee this.'

Liz wondered if Ilona ever, actually, did anything for herself. Several vulgar images flashed before her, but she put them aside and stuck to her game-plan.

Watching him carefully, silently pouring two glasses of wine, she said, 'The point is, Kit, on the night of the party you are to start seriously romancing you-know-who.'

Kit groaned.

'You must. We're running out of money. The party will be the ideal opportunity. A moonlit stroll, hand in hand, along the beach. Then your first kiss . . .'

She broke off. God, Kit really did look ready to retch. She threw back her rosé and reached for the bottle. For the first time, Liz started to have serious doubts about pulling the whole thing off.

NINE

Aᴏᴛᴇʀ ʙʀᴇᴀᴋꜰᴀsᴛ Iʟᴏɴᴀ and Paula announced they were walking into Cannes to buy gloves. In the blue-and-yellow kitchen, crumbling his croissant, Kit had found the female chatter interminable. Should they buy white cotton or nylon? Cotton was cooler but got grubby quicker. Nylon was easier to wash but didn't feel as nice.

Kit wondered why they bothered. Lizzie never wore gloves. She told him she gave it up when she went to secretarial school and sat next to a terribly 'refained' girl who had actually learned to type wearing white gloves.

When Ilona and Paula had finally cleared off he went to find Lizzie. She was in what was always known as 'Patric's library'. He owned the whole place, of course, but somehow the library spoke most of this man Kit and Liz had never met. Leather-bound books, glossy hardbacks, orange-and-white Penguins. A day bed. Leather chairs. A leather-topped desk where Liz was sitting at an old Remington typing out recipes for Paula.

'None of us can spell ratatouille.'

He came behind her and kissed the back of her neck. 'Come for a drive with me.'

Liz swivelled her chair so she was facing him. He was wearing white shorts. She longed to rip them off and have him on the carpet. But Constanza was banging around with her mop and bucket in the hall.

'You need to change, Kit. Long trousers and a jacket. We'll go into Nice.' She went on casually, 'We need to get an engagement ring for you-know-who.'

His mouth went dry. Oh God. She meant they'd got to steal the bloody thing.

As Kit directed the car down the Route de Nice Liz told him, 'We'll get an antique ring. You can say it was your mother's.'

'That went to my brother's wife. Sour-faced bitch.'

Well, OK, he hadn't exactly shone at the wedding. He had been put out because Hugh, the new Earl Rowledge, hadn't asked him to be best man. He'd chosen his fiancée's brother instead. Kit had retaliated by screwing the virgin bridesmaid in the conservatory before getting blind drunk and climbing a tree. The newly deflowered bridesmaid ran round and round the tree telling anyone in earshot that she had lost her knickers and a lot else in the conservatory.

Kit then decided it would be appropriate to decorate the tree. He took out a wad of five-pound notes and pushed them in between the leaves. He fell out of the tree and took the bridesmaid off to the morning-room for a return match. There wasn't much room as all the wedding presents were on display.

The bridesmaid was sick over a chased silver fruit stand, and somehow Kit managed to shatter a crystal decanter. Retreating towards his bedroom, he kept falling down in the corridor. Finally he was assisted to his feet by the best man, who at the door said, 'I think these are yours', and handed him a pile of five-pound notes, still leafy and twiggy.

Before he passed out Kit wondered if the pompous prune said the same thing to the bridesmaid when he returned her scanties.

In Nice Kit parked the Daimler near the Cours Saleya where they had a glass of rosé, admired Matisse's yellow house and wandered round the flower market that he had painted from his window. Then they strolled down the Promenade des Anglais, remarking on the milky blue of the sea and the way the pebble beach didn't look as kind as Cannes sand. No question of being able to afford a drink at the glamorous Negresco hotel, but Liz told Kit to slip into the men's room, admire the massive Baccarat chandelier on the way, and she would be back in fifteen minutes.

When she returned, Kit was standing outside by an absurdly garbed flunkey. He was surprised to see she was wearing a smart black straw hat.

''Struth, Lizzie. How much did that cost?'

'Tuppence, in the market. It's baloney to think you have to spend a fortune on a hat. Now pay attention. The jeweller's is up the next side road, on the right.'

'How do you know all this? Where to go, where to buy stuff?'

'I came over one time by myself, on the train. Made a note of what might be useful.' Her lips brushed his cheek. 'See you later.'

As she walked up the street Liz took from her bag a pair of white cotton gloves purchased that morning. Gloves in hand, she marched briskly into the jeweller's. As Liz expected, because she had done her research, there were two female assistants, one young and pretty, the other middle-aged.

Liz said to the latter, 'I'm looking for a ring for my sister's twenty-first. Something with a coloured stone, but I don't know what.'

'What colouring is your sister?'

Liz described Ilona. Blonde, blue eyes, long slim fingers. 'Not a bit like me!'

The young assistant was regarding her sympathetically. How awful, her expression said, to be you.

'Not rubies or emeralds,' said the older woman. 'Too heavy on blondes.' And she brought out three velvet-lined trays, one of amethysts, one of sapphires and one of aquamarines.

As Liz hovered over the rings, she heard the shop door open, and from the way the assistants stuck their chests out she knew Kit had made his entrance.

'I'm after a bracelet,' he said, in his passable French. 'Gold. For my girlfriend.'

'You want a bracelet or a bangle?' asked the young assistant.

'What's the difference?'

'A bangle is solid. Look, I'll show you.'

Liz ignored them. Her eyes were on the tray of aquamarines. One particular ring. It was a large heart-shaped stone in an art-deco setting. It was beautiful. It was the ring.

She waited. Come on, Kit. Get on with it. We talked about it long enough in the car. Still gazing at the rings, she let one of her white gloves fall to the floor.

Kit was trying bracelets and bangles on the young one, who was now all of a flirt.

Liz said to the older one, with a sigh of regret, 'Actually, I really don't think –'

There was a girlish shriek as a bangle dropped from Kit's grasp and clattered to the parquet floor. As the older woman looked sharply at them Liz took the aquamarine ring and slipped it into the glove she was holding.

'Thank you. Perhaps I'll think about it and come back.'

The woman looked daggers at her. Unhurried, Liz left the shop. Once round the corner she put on a spurt, threw the hat into a fountain and threaded her way through the back streets to the Daimler. Kit, having taken a more direct route, was there before her.

'Any problems?' she asked him.

He shook his head. 'Silly you, dropping your glove. Gallant of me to pick it up and come rushing after you.'

She slipped into his jacket pocket the glove with the ring in it and turned and made for the station. The train was slow, hot and crowded. It smelled of Gauloises and sweat. Liz had to stand up, while on the seat below her a pair of French lovers tenderly picked blackheads from one another's noses.

When she got back to the villa she found Ilona and Paula rather self-consciously modelling new bikinis.

'I've never worn one before,' Ilona said. 'What do you think, Kit?'

He regarded the four triangles of white material seemingly tied together with string. He managed to look rakish and slightly embarrassed at the same time. 'Er, charming. Absolutely.'

Liz beamed. 'I'll just go and wash my hands, and then I'll get lunch. You must be starving after such a busy morning.'

She plodded upstairs. As arranged, Kit had hidden the ring under her mattress. She removed it from the glove and did what she hadn't dared do in the jeweller's. She tried it on. It was heavenly. The heart-shaped aquamarine and the art-deco setting were masterly together. A pity it didn't suit her plump fingers. With regret she took the ring off. Found her sewing-box and took it with the ring into Kit's room.

She waved her nail scissors at the golly. 'Hello, Golly. You're going to have your appendix out.'

*

At Antibes harbour Colin was peering at the boats, trying to remember the name of Skip's. He could have asked at the *capitainerie*, but he didn't want to do that. Didn't want them remembering that he'd been here today.

His thoughts ran on in parallel. Don't forget. *Pharmacie*. Joleen's tablets. Heck, fancy old Skip getting his own boat. What the hell was it called? There must be over a hundred boats moored at Antibes. And Skip might not even be here. The point of a boat is that you go out in it.

But it was Skip, finally, who found him, attracting Colin's attention with a piercing finger whistle. 'Wotcha, cock.' He was on deck, puffing at a roll-up. He grinned as Colin clambered aboard. 'Somehow, I had a feeling you'd turn up.'

Colin said, 'Can we go below?'

Paula was alone in the hall when the phone rang. She picked it up and at the sound of his voice yelled, 'Patric! We agreed. I ring you. You don't ring me.'

'Are you alone?'

'Yes. They're at the beach, and Kit's down at the port. Constanza's in the garden bossing the pool boy.'

'I wanted to know how it went with Joleen and Colin.'

Paula gave him a run-down of the evening at the Moulin d'Or, ending with, 'I'm pretty sure Ilona's got her eye on Kit.'

'What's his response?'

'Hard to say. He's charming to everyone.'

'Well, Ilona's used to getting what she wants. Which reminds me. It's funny, but I never knew how she hooked Hans. I mean, he was a prisoner of war. Under lock and key.'

Paula wriggled on to the gilt chair next to the telephone and told him the story. How the officers were allowed to come to church on Sundays, where the helpful Girl Guides handed out the hymn books. 'So Ilona was slipping him seductive little notes at hymn number 156.'

'What's 156?'

'"Come Down O Love Divine".'

Patric roared with laughter, then said quietly, 'But you saw him first, didn't you?'

'Yes. But it was just a crush. I had them all the time.'

She paused, listening. 'That's the kitchen door. Constanza.'

'Do you approve of my kitchen?'

'I do. I like the blue and yellow, and I like those plates called Cannes.'

'You recognize them?'

'Of course. They're by Hugh Casson.'

'One day I'll bring you a peach on one of those plates. When you're in bed. When I've woken you up to make love to you.'

'Look –'

'And with regard to the kitchen, you will note that there is a table. I intend to –'

Paula rang off and went into the kitchen to say something cheery to Constanza. But she wasn't there. The person who had been there, listening intently, was Liz.

'Oh, fiddle,' Ilona had said when they got to the beach. 'I left my sunhat in the kitchen.'

So, of course, Liz had offered to trek back to the villa to fetch it. Good thing, too. So Paula was reporting to this Patric guy. And what else was going on between them? He owned the villa. He was an old friend of Ilona and her late husband. Liz hoped to God he didn't turn up. Things were going well at this end. It certainly sounded as though Kit had played a blinder at the Moulin d'Or, especially with Ilona.

Liz smiled grimly as she espied her in her red swimsuit. Got an eye on my Kit, have you? Well, don't worry, dearie. Soon he'll be charming your posh little pants off.

Paula arrived minutes later carrying, Liz noticed, nothing

more than a silk sarong. Paula had prepared the picnic. Liz and Constanza had packed it into two large hampers, which Liz had humped down to the beach. Then she came back for towels, two parasols and a straw basket containing magazines, paperbacks, sun oil – bloody kitchen sink, Liz thought crossly.

I feel like a mule. Perhaps it should be a verb. I mule, you don't mule, Liz always mules. She smiled at Paula. 'What a pretty sarong.'

'Thanks. Present from my boyfriend. Correction. Ex-boyfriend.' They were waiting, so she told them about Ben. Played it light, tried to make it funny. 'He said he couldn't come round, so I had some supper – haggis, actually (pause for laughter) and took myself off to the flicks. It was still sloshing with rain, and I was early, and there was a café next to the cinema. I went in. And there was Ben. And he didn't notice me.' Paula spread out her towel on the sand and went on, 'He didn't notice me for two reasons. One, the busty blonde he was with. Two, his plate of bacon, egg and bubble-and-squeak.'

'So he was hungry,' said Liz.

Paula shook her head. 'The point is, in all the years I knew him, Ben would never eat anything green. Not salads, peas, beans and certainly not cabbage. And I make fantastic bubble-and-squeak. But he would never, ever eat it.'

'So you knew it was serious with the blonde,' said Ilona.

Liz loved this story. Loved it. Serves her right, the snotty bitch. Then she remembered about Patric. What was going on? How often was Paula on the line in her room, murmuring sweet nothings? If only, Liz thought, she could get rid of Constanza and Ilona she might be able to pick up the hall phone and listen in.

Paula was saying to Ilona, 'Of course, I was away at catering school when you ran off with Hans. I've forgotten ... how did you manage to give your parents the slip?'

'Easy-peasy. Mummy had been ill, and Daddy took her to America on a cruise. I told Daddy I'd go and stay with the Guide captain, but I didn't. I stayed in the house and waited for Hans.'

'You knew he was coming,' said Liz, resigning herself to hearing the story yet again.

Ilona smoothed on coconut oil. 'Before he was sent home, the last time at the church, he left a note for me in the hymn book. He said he would come back for me. And he did. One Sunday morning. I came out of church, and he was waiting, in a huge Mercedes. He said get in, so I did and he drove to the ferry and then to Dover.'

'You mean you just went,' prompted Liz dutifully.

'I just went. I remembered that's what Colin Love did when he took off with Joleen. We were all terribly impressed. When I did it, the neighbours got word to my parents. They were furious, of course, but they were in the middle of the Atlantic. Eventually they managed to notify the police, but by then Hans and I were across the Channel.'

Paula knew they had withheld their permission for their daughter to marry. But the following year Ilona was eighteen and free. Her father disinherited her, and so what? Hans's industrialist family was loaded, and he was already a millionaire.

'Patric Ryan tried to patch things up between me and my parents, but Daddy wouldn't have it. He's been a tower of strength, Patric. Done a lot of legal work for us. He's very discreet.'

So I was right, thought Paula. Publishing's just a front. Patric is an international lawyer with a clutch of powerful clients. No wonder he could afford to buy me a kitchen table. I should have asked for a gold rolling-pin as well.

Liz had embarked on what she told Kit later was the 'ammo initiative'.

'The more information we've got on you-know-who, the more ammunition we've got if things get tricky.'

'So you never regretted marrying so young, Ilona?'

Liz learned again that Ilona had fallen for Hans the instant she first saw him, and, no, she had never regretted marrying him. That said, there were aspects of life at the Schloss that irked her: the formal dinners she had to give, and the bodyguard Hans insisted went with her whenever she left the estate alone.

'We had eleven very happy years together. Then he got this lung infection and started to go downhill. I was frantic. And then he rallied. The doctors were amazed. I was able to take him away, to Gstaad. It was wonderful. We had little walks or sat on our balcony in the sun, all cosy. I was supposed to learn to ski, but I was such a duffer, falling over all the time, I thought Hans was never going to stop laughing.'

Neither Paula nor Liz were fooled for a second by this. Ilona was a natural athlete. Skiing would have been a breeze for her. But she didn't want to disappear up a mountain and leave her husband alone.

'And then when we came back,' her voice broke, 'he died. Suddenly. In his sleep. He never said goodbye.'

Paula was rummaging in a hamper and brought out a bottle of what had once contained Tizer. She poured three glasses and handed one to Ilona.

At the first sip the distress on her face melted. 'Lemonade! You've made lemonade. Like we used to take on our picnics, Paula. Do you remember, we used to go blackberrying and Cook would make blackberry-and-apple jam. Do you remember the smell? Oh,' she was peering into the second hamper, 'and you've made blancmange! Chocolate blancmange in little cups. I haven't had that since I left home. They don't do it in Germany.'

'Don't do it here either. I had to bring it with me from London' – along with the Marmite, HP sauce, tomato soup and breakfast tea you had already got from the English shop down the road.

Liz was wondering if she could face lunch. The inter-mingling smells of their childhood jam, the chocolate blancmange, the strong, sweetish scent of the coconut oil worn by everyone on the beach, they were all whirling unpleasant messages to her stomach.

Still, the lemonade was delicious, and she had to admit Paula's idea of picnic food was miles away from the slapped-together sandwiches Liz would have provided.

Paula had bought two *bagnats*, sliced the tops off and removed the inner bread. Into one she fitted a cold cheese omelette and the other she filled with sliced chicken, ham and olives. Then the bread lids were put back on and the *bagnats* were left to chill in the fridge overnight. This morning she had cut them into wedges and wrapped them in greaseproof paper. Also in the hamper were halved tomatoes, pepper, salt and cherries.

'Say cheese!' It was Joleen, aiming her camera. She was wearing an acid-yellow swimsuit and clanking with enough jewellery, Paula thought, to regild Lady Docker's silver Daimler. Paula also noticed the very wide shoulder straps on the swimsuit, presumably to hide the scar they knew Joleen was left with after a car crash years ago.

Just before the camera clicked, Ilona grabbed a towel and threw it over her head. She said, muffled, 'I hate having my picture taken.'

'I never knew that,' Paula said, as Ilona emerged from the towel.

'I never seem to stand up straight. Or I'm pulling a face. It's all right for you, Paula. You're naturally photo-genic.'

Fancy, thought Liz. One of the most celestial women on earth, and she worries she goes all wonky in photos. Liz said sociably to Joleen, 'Where's Colin?'

'Why is it, Liz,' Joleen said frostily, 'that you have such a thing for my Col?'

Oh hell, thought Liz. She thinks I'm making a play for her husband.

'Come off it, Joleen,' laughed Ilona. 'You're always saying, Colin, where have you *been*? Where is he anyway?'

'Yes, what have you done with our Colin?' Paula joined in.

'I don't know where he is. And I don't care. He went into Antibes the other day to get some tablets I need and completely forgot! Pretended it was lunchtime and the drugstore was shut.'

Paula mentioned the *pharmacie* near the harbour in Cannes, and Joleen went into a rant. 'D'you think I'm some knucklehead? D'you think I haven't been there? Gave them the name of the pills, and they looked at me like I was crazy. Said they couldn't be got in France.'

That's the French all over, thought Paula. When they don't understand, it's a shrug and a *non*. And what I don't understand is what's wrong with Joleen. When she was younger she was feisty, and it was very attractive. Look at the way she took on that terrible father when the bully was belting Colin. But she's not a teenager any more. Now she's older that old fighting spirit is turning her into a harridan.

Joleen was now shouting at Ilona, 'No, of course I couldn't describe what the pills are for. How do you mime cystitis?'

Ilona shut up. She had never suffered from cystitis. And she could see Kit strolling towards them down the beach.

Paula rejected the idea of making a joke about it being honeymoonitis and said, 'If you've got a few pills left and the packet, see what the ingredients are. They might respond better to that in the *pharmacie*.'

'I've had cystitis,' said Liz. 'It's agony. Burns when you wee, and I couldn't even walk properly. I didn't know you could get tablets. I just lay in a cold bath, for days.'

Joleen got to her feet. 'Good idea. I've gotta do something. I'm desperate.'

She walked – somewhat awkwardly they noticed – to the water's edge. Just as she was about to wade in Kit came racing up the beach, grabbed Joleen and pulled her towards him. She fought him and was about to sink her teeth into his restraining arm when he threw her down on the sand.

Liz couldn't look. Ilona and Paula had rushed to help Joleen get up.

'Sorry,' Kit said. 'But look.' He pointed to the water.

They all regarded him blankly, except Joleen who looked ready to murder him.

'Those pretty violet things shimmying about. Jellyfish. Get stung by one of those and it's like being badly burned.'

Instead of thanking Kit, Joleen marched up to Liz. 'This is all your fault! I could have died in there. You –'

'Hold on,' Kit said firmly. 'When you swim off the yacht, don't you have to look out for jellyfish? You must have seen them.'

'As a matter of fact, I don't swim,' Joleen muttered. 'I never learned.'

'Well, don't ever speak to Lizzie like that again. D'you hear?'

'Lunch,' Paula said. 'At once, don't you think?'

TEN

THE BIKINIS' FIRST public appearance was going to be in St-Tropez. By the time the villa party arrived at the *Lovebite II* Joleen and Colin were into their first spat of the day.

'For God's sake, Joleen, keep away from the bridge. Knut's got to sail the bloody boat.'

'I merely asked if he'd like some fresh orange juice.'

'If he wants juice he'll get one of the crew to fetch it.'

Joleen, wearing a pink polka-dot playdress, flounced off to greet her guests. 'Oh good. You haven't brought *her*.'

Kit strolled to the rail and pretended to admire the view. He had begged Liz to come. Pleaded; almost wept. When she wasn't there to keep the show on the road he felt so vulnerable. But she was adamant, insisting that she was not going to spend the entire voyage throwing up, and anyway she loathed Joleen.

As the boat left the Bay of Cannes and Knut ordered the Blue Peter run down from the foremast, Joleen had breakfast served on the sundeck. Apart from the fresh orange juice there was coffee, tea, croissants, white and brown rolls, Normandy butter, three types of *confiture* plus a dish of peaches and apricots.

When Ilona and Paula slipped off their sarongs, Joleen screamed. 'Bikinis! I haven't got one! They've been banned for years in the States. Oh, oh!'

The wailing went on so long Ilona suggested she pick one up in St-Tropez.

Colin gave a hollow laugh. 'You know what they say about St Trop. Everything's too much.'

'If I have a bikini,' Joleen frowned, 'it will show my scar.'

The car-crash scar at the top of her back was certainly impressive, but Ilona and Paula reassured her and restored her to her usual fiery self.

From Cannes the *Lovebite* headed out past the ancient red rocks of the Esterel mountains. Paula had the Cadogan guidebook open:

> The Esterel mountains are supposed to receive their name from the fairy Esterelle, who intoxicates and deceives her ardent lovers and thus fittingly makes her home on the Coast of Illusion.
>
> Between Cannes and St-Raphael this fairy coast of illusion provides one of nature's strangest but most magnificent interludes. A wild massif of blood-red cliffs tumbling into the blue, blue sea.

Beyond St-Raphael the mountains of the Massif des Maures came into view as one of the crew arrived with a message from the bridge. 'Skipper says keep an eye to port, sir,' he said to Colin.

They all rushed to the left side of the boat, and there they were, just ahead: six dolphins playing in the water. Knut slowed the boat, Joleen took photographs and Kit wished Liz was here to share the experience with him.

He sighed. Still, better get on with it. He touched Ilona's bare arm. 'Magic, isn't it?'

Smiling, she took off her sunglasses. My God, he thought.

Her eyes were big enough and blue enough to sail a boat in.

'Come on, girls, make yourself decent. We're nearly there,' Colin said, as Knut turned the *Lovebite*'s bows towards the most famous fishing village in the world.

Dusky pink-and-ochre houses, quayside cafés, desperate artists cursing Matisse, Bonnard and Signac, who got to the golden-lit village first and did a better job.

'Why do we have to cover up when all you've come for, Colin, is to see Brigitte Bardot swimming naked.'

Colin grinned at Kit. 'Her villa's just up the road. We could stroll up there.'

'Great idea.'

As they turned away from the glaring Joleen, Colin said, 'Did you see that film?'

And God Created Woman. You bet Kit had seen it. That Bardot was his kind of woman. Great tits and a great arse. Not a bag of bones like the one he'd got to marry.

'Did you see they sacked Jane in the *Daily Mirror*? She was a bit of all right,' said Kit.

When they got back they selected a quayside brasserie to wait for the girls. They ordered beers and gazed out across the port at the *Lovebite*.

'Terrific boat, Colin. Just what I'd like. If ever I had a yacht.'

Colin looked puzzled. 'But you did have one. She was called *Audrey*. You told us that night at the Moulin d'Or.'

Blast. Liz would kill him. He took a pull of his beer and grimaced. 'To be honest, I mean, to be totally frank with you, I try to forget I ever owned *Aud*. Came to a sticky end, you see. I ran her aground off Antigua.'

'Christ. Bad luck. Actually, well, to be honest with you

I'm not sure how much longer we'll keep the yacht. It's so bloody expensive. But don't say a word to the wife.'

When the girls arrived, Joleen was in a good mood. She'd bought a red bikini and some leather gladiator sandals. 'Did you see BB?'

'Yeah, she invited us in,' said Colin. 'We had a three-some.'

Paula said, 'She was in *Doctor at Sea* with Dirk Bogarde.'

'She wasn't,' said Colin.

'Was.'

'*Wasn't.*'

And, as often happened, they were kids again, back at the Isle of Wight caff. Unlike Liz, Kit didn't mind all this. He wished he'd been there. Sounded fun.

'It's the phrases your parents used,' Ilona was saying, 'and you swore you never would, and then as you get older . . .'

'Take your jacket off,' Joleen told Colin, 'or you won't feel the benefit when you go out.'

'Stick to your last. Jack of all trades, master of none.'

'Masturbation makes you go blind.'

'Is she going out looking like that?'

Paula pointed. 'Oh, look. A marching band. How jolly.'

Kit was not feeling jolly. He was staring in disbelief at a group of people just behind the band. A man, a woman and three young daughters. It was his brother Hugh with his family.

Despite the midday heat, Kit froze. He hadn't seen his brother since the horror of the wedding. To be fair, Hugh had been most apologetic about not having Kit as best man, explaining that Annabel had insisted on it being her brother. Then, after the bridesmaid incident and the money-in-the-tree incident and the morning-room incident, Annabel had banned him from the house.

Hell, they were obviously looking for somewhere to have lunch. Kit doubted if his sister-in-law would acknowledge him, but Hugh would. Kit would be obliged to do the honours. 'May I introduce the Earl and Countess Rowledge', and Joleen would immediately invite them to the party at the villa. Liz would be there. Hugh would know that Liz had never worked for their father, the old earl, and had certainly not met Kit at the house. Hugh and Annabel would know that he had never owned a yacht. It all went on and on.

He bolted inside and went to think things through in the WC. Footprint job. Not enough to put the girls off. They were used to it in the bars near the Cannes port.

Even so, it gave him an idea.

As he shot out of the brasserie he saw his brother and the family crossing the road towards the villa party. They still hadn't seen him. Annabel was fussing with the children, and Hugh, despite the spectacles, could never see more than two yards in front of him.

With his back to his family Kit yanked Paula to her feet. 'Come on, everyone. We must leave. I've just seen into the kitchen. Disgusting. I can't let you eat here. You'd end up in hospital!' He managed to shoo them all out just in time.

But Joleen refused to go any further than the next place on the quay. 'This sandal keeps slipping. Colin will have to fix it.'

They settled into the wicker chairs. Kit took a seat furthest away from the family group at the next-door brasserie. He saw Annabel glancing around. He bent down to look at Joleen's gladiator sandal. 'Let me help you with that.' Mayday, mayday. Annabel was looking this way. She was saying something to Hugh, and he was getting up.

Where can I run to? WC? No, Hugh could follow me in. Trap me. Cigarettes? It was lunchtime. All the *tabacs* were shut.

Just as he was trying to hide behind Joleen's sandal, the marching band stopped playing and a shot rang out. Then it became an ear-splitting fusillade as more shots were fired into the stone pavement. Through the acrid smoke and screaming women Kit could see a crowd of young men in quaint soldiers' uniforms. They carried blunderbusses and were enjoying themselves hugely, blazing away like madmen and turning all the bystanders into choking wrecks.

'COLIN!'

He took Joleen in his arms. 'It's all right. It's just stupid boys making a stupid noise.'

Paula wiped her stinging eyes. 'It's the Bravade des Espagnols. I read about it in the book this morning. Commemorates the time the St-Trops saw off a fleet of Spanish galleys.'

'Hell's teeth,' said Ilona. 'They're going to do it all over again.'

'Colin, *do* something!'

There was no need for Colin to do anything. As the boy soldiers assumed their firing positions Annabel was on her feet. 'Stop that! Stop it this instant! How dare you frighten my girls like that.'

The boys glowered at her. They did not understand English but could recognize a mad Englishwoman when she confronted them.

Then the leader shrugged, gave an order, and the boys raised their muskets.

Annabel snapped her fingers at her husband. 'Come along, Hugh. We'll get the girls back to the car.'

'Crazy to drive down here,' commented Colin. 'The road's always jammed.'

Ilona was observing Annabel. 'Three daughters. And she's pregnant. Did you notice?'

'Keeping old Hugh at it until he comes up with a boy,' laughed Joleen.

Got it in one, thought Kit. If anything happened to Hugh the earldom could not pass to a daughter. If there was no son, next in line was Kit. Which, of course, for Annabel was too appalling to contemplate.

They lunched on grilled fish and *frites*, followed by a Cointreau soufflé so delicious that Paula invaded the kitchen to beg for the recipe. Then Joleen changed into her new bikini, and they headed for the beach.

The *Lovebite II* sailed back into Cannes just as it was getting dark. It was always a stirring moment, thought Kit, coming into a port, but Cannes was so entrancing it was a very special arrival. The harbour lights glittered, and across the bay they could see, like silver tinsel, the glimmer from Théoule. Annoyingly, in view of The Plan, it wasn't Ilona standing next to him but Paula, doing her talking-guidebook thing.

'You can see, can't you, Kit, why they call it the Riviera. The lights are like diamond necklaces. *Rivière* is an old French word for necklace.'

He walked Ilona and Paula back to the villa. Liz had laid the terrace table and was lighting citronella candles.

'I thought you'd probably have fish for lunch, so I made a chicken casserole.'

'Smells wonderful,' said Kit, although all he could smell was citronella.

It was wonderful.

'I'm so impressed,' Paula said. 'I'd never have thought of putting stuffed olives in a chicken casserole.'

'I just used what there was at the market. There's cheese and salad afterwards.'

When they'd finished Kit helped Liz stack the plates in the kitchen ready for Constanza to wash up in the morning. She gave him a come-to-bed look. Immediately he returned to the terrace, smothered a yawn and said, 'I think I'll – er – just get my head down.'

Liz finished clearing the table, hung around in the kitchen for a bit and then went to say goodnight to Ilona and Paula.

'I won't be far behind you,' said Paula. 'All that fresh air's exhausting.'

Liz got to her room and was just about to strip off ready for Kit when there was a tap at the door. She frowned. What was he playing at? Usually he walked straight in.

She flung open the door, and there was Ilona.

'Sorry to disturb you. I wanted to give you this.' She held out a small package, tied with emerald ribbon.

'Goodness! Come in,' Liz said, leaving the door open so Kit would see she had a visitor.

They sat on the bed. Liz tore off the wrapping and opened a small box. It contained a coral ring. 'Oh how pretty!'

'They had lots of coral in St-Tropez. Such a pity you couldn't come, so I thought I'd get you this to make up for it a bit. Let's try it on.'

I want a fuck, thought Liz, not a frilly girly chat. Thank heavens I did a filling meal. Otherwise she might be wanting a midnight feast, à la bleeding Girl Guides. She thanked Ilona effusively, speaking as loudly as she dared so that Kit would hear and keep away.

Suddenly Ilona was laughing. 'You brought him in here!' She was pointing at the golly. 'I suppose you thought Kit wouldn't really want to sleep in the same room as a stuffed toy.'

Ha-ha, went Liz. Ha-ha, went Ilona. And finally the door shut behind her.

Liz regarded her coral ring, then looked at the golly. 'Well, well,' she said.

'What did she want?' Kit asked, locking the door.

She showed him the ring. 'Present.' She pulled him towards the bed, tugging off his white shorts. 'Oh come here. I've missed you, lover. Missed you so much.'

As she went to work on him Kit wondered, as he often did, where she had learned it all. When he'd asked her, early in their relationship, she just said, 'Oh, for my job I have to scan a lot of continental magazines. They tell you far more than the English ones.' And she'd added casually, 'The French seem barmy about buggery.'

Now, she washed her hands and poured two glasses of water from the jug on the wash-stand. 'Don't go to sleep. I want to know how it went today. Did you make any headway?'

Kit didn't think touching Ilona's arm counted as headway. 'It was difficult. Such a crowd. And you weren't there, and things kept happening.'

He gave her an account of the day, editing out the BB episode, which he knew she would dismiss as juvenile.

Liz listened aghast to the Hugh and Annabel near-miss. She had never met them and hoped she never would. Poor Kit, having to deal with it all on his own. She'd go to the *pharmacie* tomorrow and ask for seasickness tablets, like the ones you got for car journeys: Kwells.

She smoothed back Kit's hair and with her cool hands stroked his eyebrows and around his eyes. He always liked that. 'Now listen. We have to work out how you're going to propose to you-know-who.'

Kit moaned.

'I'm serious. You can't make a mess of it, and you can't leave her in any doubt about what you're asking. And you can't say anything like, "If I asked you to marry me what would you say?"'

'I'm not worried about the words. It's a question of where I say them. If we're in the villa garden someone might come barging up. I suppose I could take her for a moonlit walk on the beach.'

Liz considered and vetoed this. It might start raining. Or if it was a night of crashing waves they might drown out his passionate little speech. 'What was that you said, Kit?' 'I said, I LOVE YOU.' '*What*?' What a farce.

'I think you'd be better off in the car. You'd be more in control. When they go out one day we'll drive along the coast. Find a suitable place for you to park . . . Kit! Are you listening?'

He had fallen asleep.

'The noise was dreadful.'

'You just went on the wrong day. Be even worse on Liberation Day. The whole place is roaring with jeeps and tanks. It's to commemorate the Yanks freeing the south of France from the Germans. Churchill was there, watching from a destroyer.'

Paula yawned.

'Oh, sorry,' Patric snapped. 'How boring that the French Resistance were incredibly brave –'

'Look. I had to leave my mother. I was an evacuee. I had to stand in a line with my label, my ration book and my gas mask. I had to stand there and wait to be chosen.'

'Well, you did all right. Why did Ilona choose you?'

'I don't know. I was just relieved I wasn't left till last.'

'Are you still wearing that bikini?'

'Yes.' They hadn't bothered to change for supper.

'Take it off.'

Paula sighed. Men! You spent a fortune on pretty scanties and all they ever wanted was to get you stripped off. Obediently, she wriggled out of the bikini. She could have pretended, of course, read a magazine and filed her nails, but somehow Patric always seemed to know.

'I'm going to start at your feet, and I'm going to kiss you all the way up your legs, and I'm going to open your legs and carry on kissing you –'

Paula came. Just like that. And loudly. Damn you, she thought. Damn you, Patric Ryan.

'That's promising,' he said. 'I'd rather see it for real,

though. If I could see your face I'd know whether you were concentrating on me or that boyfriend of yours.'

'That is all over.'

'What happened?'

'None of your business.'

'It is. I want to know all about you.'

She told him about the haggis, and the blonde and the bubble-and-squeak. 'I mean, it shows he'd been seeing her for some time, doesn't it? If it was all new he'd want to impress, take her somewhere like the Ritz.'

'Are you still in love with him?'

'No.'

'Sure?'

'I'll prove it.' She fetched from the bureau her loose-leaf folder. She took out the holiday snap of her and Ben on a Welsh beach. She looked at it one last time. Then holding it near the phone, she tore it into bits.

'Did you hear that? I just shredded Ben.'

In one of his frequent conversational swerves (she guessed he must have been an ace rugby player) he said, 'You never told me how you got on with the haggis. Cooking it with carrots.'

'It was great.' Paula was not going to admit that she'd sat at her table in floods of self-pity because deep down she already knew that Ben had left her. 'How does an Irishman know that? Carrots if you can't find swede?'

'This particular Irishman has a Scottish girlfriend.'

And then Paula felt it. The first lethal stab of jealousy. Hell, I've just torn up Ben's picture, and now he's telling me about his girlfriend. How lousy is that?

'She's what you might call a friendly fuck. We've known each other a long time.'

Paula was listening carefully. 'I'd better go. I said I'd look in on Ilona.'

'Be careful not to use her bathroom.'

They'd already laughed about this, the garish black-and-red tiled bathroom that had been chosen by Patric's grandfather.

'I'll call you after the party.'

'No. I'm going away for a week. I'll be off the radar.'

'Why? Don't they have telephones in Scotland?'

'I'm going to Ireland. Going to steal a bike and visit some old haunts.'

He means he's going to look up old girlfriends, Paula thought, as she put the phone down.

ELEVEN

Paula curled up on the bed and thought about how they first met. That soggy day. The ladies' room at Fortnum's, surprisingly resembling the interior of a tart's spongebag. Checking her hair looked good, regretting her sopping court shoes, entering the restaurant. Seeing Patric for the first time, rising to his feet, the Celtic good looks – and then, lying on his bed at the Villa Fleurie, Paula couldn't restrain herself any longer.

She cut to the kiss. Relived every second. His right hand grabbing her hair, his left holding her shoulder, his mouth sweetish with fine wine, and the tenderness and the rising passion, and her own mouth, her own body, betraying her.

Then that first phone call. The direct way he'd just said, 'I'll come and fuck you across your kitchen table.'

It could have been offensive. He could have said *embrace* or *make love*, but the earthiness of it made it very sexy, in retrospect. Paula was annoyed with herself now for her lack of response. I got all prim. But he caught me on the hop.

She went over all she knew about this man from her own research before she met him and what he'd told her down the phone.

Elegant French mother, ebullient Irish father. Mother preferred Paris to the south of France, so Patric's holidays were spent either in Ireland or in Cannes with his grandparents. Read law at Trinity College, Dublin. Enjoyed sailing, rugby. Married. Divorced three years later. No children. Homes in Cannes and Chelsea, London. Member of White's and Chelsea Arts Club. Had 'drifted', he said, into publishing after the war, but Paula now knew that was a front. He was a top international lawyer, a highly paid trouble-shooter appreciated for his skills and his discretion.

And he had a Scottish girlfriend.

And Paula was falling in love with him.

And he was messing her about.

'I don't understand,' Paula said to Ilona. 'How can I be so obsessed with a man I've met only once?'

She and Ilona were having lunch under the trees at the Café des Allées in Cannes. On the bandstand the orchestra was just striking up.

'I can tell you why,' said Ilona. It was, she said, all to do with separation. 'You first meet someone, and, whether you're admitting it or not, you find him attractive. Then, for one reason or another, you don't meet again. Years ago, in countries like Spain, this was deliberate. The couple were given one chaperoned meeting, usually one Sunday, and then the girl was locked up until the guy came round to ask formal permission to pay court to her.'

The waitress came with a bottle of rosé, a carafe of water, a basket of bread and a dish of black olives. Ilona poured herself some water, still with the imprisoned Spanish girl. 'She thinks about him constantly. She goes over everything he said, the way he looked at her, the sound of his voice . . .'

Paula threw back half a glass of wine. This was beginning to sound horribly familiar.

The point was, Ilona went on, that during this period of separation the girl built the man up to heroic heights. In her mind he became taller, more handsome, more virile. 'He's going through the same enhancement with her. She's prettier, her eyelashes are longer, her hair's more lustrous, her figure's more enticing.'

'Seems like an elaborate way of saying absence makes the heart grow fonder,' said Paula. 'You'd think after all this anticipation when they do meet again they'd crash with disappointment.'

'No, no. They are on fire. Absolutely scorching for one another. Because the person they are seeing is the one they have been imagining.'

'OK, OK,' Paula groaned. 'How do you know so much about lovesick women?'

'It's not me. It's Stendhal. He wrote a whole book about how people fall in love.'

Paula was amazed. Ilona had been sporty at school, not academic. Certainly not the type to stretch out on the sofa with Stendhal. She said as much.

'Oh well, I had to have something to do in that gloomy Schloss.'

'Will you sell it?'

'Not mine to sell. Hans wanted it kept in the family, so he's left it to a cousin. I couldn't care less.'

The waitress arrived. Paula had chosen for them Salade Niçoise Ravigote, made with julienne strips of chicken instead of tuna.

'Delicious dressing,' said Ilona, tucking in. 'What's in it?'

Paula told her it was ravigote sauce, made with chopped tarragon, watercress, chives, garlic, parsley, mustard, wine vinegar and olive oil. She was going to put it in her book.

'How's it going?'

'OK. But collecting the recipes is the easy bit. Testing the damn things takes ages.'

They were eating late after coffee, croissants and fruit with Joleen on the yacht. Then when the shops opened again at four they were going shopping for party dresses.

'For pity's sake, can't you get that Liz into something decent?' Joleen had said over breakfast. 'That striped thing she had on at the beach made her look like a deckchair. Where does she find clothes so huge and so hideous?'

Ilona had already offered to take Liz shopping and buy her something for the party, and Liz had flatly said no thanks. Liz had learned years ago never to go shopping with girlfriends – especially when one of them looked like Grace Kelly.

Sensing the problem, Paula told her how, when she was doing her Cordon Bleu course, she wanted to treat herself to the type of beautifully cut jacket worn by the chic French. The assistant disappeared into the back of the shop and reappeared with a jacket that fitted perfectly and looked fantastic. Even so, Paula wasn't sure. As she said to Liz, she just wanted the fun of trying things on. She pointed to another jacket on the rail and asked to try it. The assistant ignored her. She asked again. The assistant stared out of the window.

'Why didn't you just snatch the jacket and put it on?' asked Liz.

'Couldn't. It was one of those shops where everything's chained up. Anyway, I got nasty. Shouted. And she pointed to the jacket and sneered, "You want to put *zat* on your bodee?" I said, yes, I did want to put *zat* on my bodee, so she unchained it, and I put it on and it looked frightful.'

Over breakfast, Paula had told Joleen the story. 'I was trying to get through to Liz that a French *vendeuse* won't let you out of the shop looking like shit.'

It hadn't worked. Liz adamantly refused to accompany them.

Joleen said, 'Why don't you just buy her a tablecloth and she can make a skirt out of it.'

'Actually,' said Ilona, 'that's an idea. There's a sewing machine at the villa. If we got a length of silk –'

'No, it's a drag to machine,' said Joleen. 'She'd have to do it by hand. Take ages. Taffeta or grosgrain would be better.'

Joleen then insisted on Colin driving her into Nice to look for her dress.

'Poor old Colin,' said Paula, as she and Ilona finished their lunch. 'Trawling round dress shops, in the heat. And she doesn't need another frock. One of the cabins is stuffed with them. I don't know what's happening in that marriage. She's absolutely vile to him.' She was starting to feel more cheerful. She'd had a thought. Perhaps Patric wasn't really going to Ireland. Perhaps . . . he was planning to come to the party.

Ilona was gazing at a stylish girl wearing a white top pulled down over one shoulder. 'We could get Lizzie a top like that. She's got nice shoulders.'

Early that morning Liz had eased her nice shoulders under Kit's mosquito net and done interesting things to him with the golly. Then she lay back and informed him that they had to think about his honeymoon.

'I can't go through with it,' said Kit. 'Not unless you're close.'

'I realize that. My first thought was for you to sweep her off to somewhere totally exotic. But it would be expensive, and I don't know if I could find a good enough excuse to turn up somewhere like Bora-Bora.'

A better plan, Liz told him, was for 'you two lovebirds' to honeymoon in London. Liz had established that, having grown up on the Isle of Wight, Ilona had never been to London. 'You'll stay at the Ritz, and I'll get a room over the road in Shepherd Market.'

'Liz, that's a red-light district.'

'I know. What fun. You can nip over and tell me how it's going, and I'll plan your itinerary. The Café de Paris certainly, but she'd probably like to go out of town as well. A cosy country pub, with horse brasses – where are you going?' She demanded, as Kit slid out of bed.

'La Bocca market. See if I can get Paula some water-cress.'

Liz didn't offer to go with him. The less they were seen together the better. It was risky Liz coming to his room, Kit thought, as he left the villa, but he couldn't do without her. Just couldn't.

He enjoyed the mile-long walk down the route de Fréjus, past villas splashed with pink and purple bougainvillaea and balustraded walls painterly with blue convolvuluses. La Bocca was a small, untouristy town to the west of Cannes that Kit had taken to exploring, since he was sure it was one place where he wouldn't run into his brother.

He had become fond of La Bocca. He particularly liked the charming little houses with cottage-style gardens, bright with flowers and fecund with climbing beans, cabbages, garlic and fennel. Most had their own lemon or orange trees, but there were orchards, too, for apples, pears and plums and well-tended market gardens that Kit realized supplied the major market in Cannes.

He sat by a dry riverbed, on a grass verge brilliant with poppies; surprising for June, but he'd noticed that in La Bocca flowers and shrubs bloomed later than in Cannes, perhaps because the little town had a particular climate that made it slightly cooler than its big sister down the road.

He was thinking with mounting gloom beyond the

honeymoon and wondering where Ilona would want to live. They were all aware that Germany had been ruled out. Paula was batting for London and Joleen for New York. Kit didn't like huge cities and certainly didn't relish Joleen as a neighbour. Not that anyone had bothered to consult him about Ilona's future living arrangements, because, of course, no one except Liz knew he was shortly to become her fiancé.

What Kit really wanted was to live in La Cachette, a sweet little house in his sightline from the grass verge. It had a Provençal tiled roof, yellow-ochre walls and blue shutters. Not in a million years could he imagine Ilona wanting to live there.

But Lizzie and I could. We could have a dog. I'd get a job, I'd do anything. A little house like that in La Bocca wouldn't cost much to rent.

He thought back to the laughs they'd had when she taught him to dance. 'Ilona will expect it,' she'd said, unwrapping the Victor Silvester records. They came with footprint charts, and written on the footprints it said 'Slow, Slow, Quick, Quick, Slow'.

'Now look, Kit. Dancing's a doddle. You just put all your weight on one leg. Now if all your weight is on your right leg, what are you going to do with your left? Correct. You've got to move it, so now you can put all your weight on your left leg. That's dancing.'

Well, despite Victor Silvester's best endeavours, Kit never mastered the foxtrot or quickstep. But he could waltz, do the Charleston and jive. It was enough. In fact, he thought it was pretty damned impressive for someone with no musical ear and very little sense of rhythm.

He glanced at his watch. Time was knocking on. The market packed up at midday. He'd be too late for Paula's watercress. Just have to say there wasn't any.

He went into his favourite café near the market where,

however glorious the weather, the locals always sat inside, playing cards and dominoes. There was the usual pungent smell of coffee, Gauloises and drains. Across the road from the market was a little row of useful shops. A *tabac*, baker, butcher, fishmonger, *pharmacie*. I could be like the French guys, Kit thought. Stroll down with the dog on Sunday morning, pick up the bread, get a cooked chicken, take it all home to Liz.

And I can't. I can't do any of that. I've got to marry fucking Ilona.

TWELVE

'COLIN! WHAT ARE you *doing* in there?' Joleen hammered on the toilet door.

'What do you think I'm doing? Embroidery?'

Joleen slammed round their cabin. Sorry, stateroom. It was too bad of Colin to get one of his upset stomachs on the night of the villa party. It meant all the time she had been trying to get ready she'd had to suffer the sound of Colin energetically working the foot pump that flushed the toilet.

Colin, of course, didn't call it a toilet; he called it 'the head', which struck Joleen as crude. The toilets, she had to admit, were one of the things she most disliked about the *Lovebite*. When you'd finished all that business with the foot pump it suddenly flushed with a frightening roar so that everyone – the crew, everyone – knew what you'd been doing. It was not that she was shy about bodily functions, Joleen told herself. You couldn't be if you were raised in a trailer. No hot water and a strip wash at the kitchen sink. It was just, well, she didn't think it was fitting for the crew to hear all the noises of the owner of the yacht on the can.

Her new dress was laid out on the bed. She had finally

tracked down what she wanted at an Italian shop in Nice. Dark-green silk, calf length, edged with white. She sat on the edge of the bed to contemplate what jewellery to wear. There was an easy chair in the stateroom, but Joleen never sat on it. Even after all these affluent years she couldn't get used to having a padded chair in a bedroom.

She regarded the dress. She had bought a white silk camellia, but, really, was that enough? Her gold necklace and bangles, and, of course, her gold cocktail watch, would look striking against the green, but the pearl necklace might blend better with the camellia.

Colin poked his head out of the toilet door. 'How's it going?'

'Oh God! Why do you always say how's it going when what you mean is hurry up?'

'OK then. So shift your arse.'

'Don't you speak to me like that. I'm not the one who's been locked in the john for the past hour.' She noticed he was holding a paperback. 'Have you been sitting in there reading?'

Colin sighed. It was difficult explaining to Joleen that the one bad thing about a boat was the lack of privacy. The head was the only place. '*Tender Is the Night*. It's good. This guy, he says wants to give a really "bad" party – as in behaviour . . .'

Joleen snatched the book from him. 'Has it got a happy ending?'

'Why do you always do that? Turn to the end first.'

'Because, you don't realize how anxious I get about every-thing. I get anxious about how I look, about all the arrange-ments I have to make on the boat, all the arrangements I have to make to keep New York and London running smoothly. I even get anxious, believe it or not, that you might leave me. I can't take on yet more anxiety worrying that a book hasn't got a happy ending.'

As Colin retreated she called to him to bring her a glass of champagne. She got up to put her dress on and yelled as she hit her head on the wooden panelling above. She did this most days because she'd insisted on a fashionable raised bed, not realizing there would be so little head-room. As Colin came in with the champagne she said, 'That goddamn ceiling. I did it again. Next time we must have a higher ceiling.'

'Next time?'

'Our next boat.' She took a handful of pills and threw them down with a gulp of champagne.

'Is that wise?' said Colin.

'I have *cystitis*, Colin. I am not going through this party in agony.'

Colin backed off and went to visit the crew heads. It was going to be a long night.

Paula was sitting on the castellated terrace outside her bedroom. She pinched off a dead leaf from one of the geraniums. She could imagine Patric relaxing here, look-ing down on the lavender near the pool and the white and pink oleanders.

For Paula it was an ideal vantage point from which to observe her worker bees arriving along the drive. Ilona had said she wanted everything kept simple, so no elaborate flower arrangements were needed. Ilona had picked garden blooms and arranged them in Provençal jugs for the buffet table under the pergola on the terrace.

Just speeding up the drive in his shooting brake was Pierre. Tall, blond with a captivating smile, he would be running the bar. His pretty dark-haired wife had come this afternoon to help with the food. She apologized for having to bring her ten-year-old daughter, Marie-Laure, but there was no one at home to care for her.

'Come on,' Paula said to the girl. 'You can help me dress the salmon with cucumber.'

Marie-Laure didn't find this at all diverting, preferring to explore underneath the hedge near the garden gate, where Constanza told her there were kittens.

Paula had decided to do the party food herself. It was what she was used to, and with her training she'd only get irritable watching a hired caterer getting it wrong. Apart from the salmon, she had cold chicken and ham, with jacket potatoes, which Pierre's wife would halve with chives and cream. There were salads, crusty bread, cheeses and for dessert fresh apricot tart, an apple charlotte and an iced coffee cake.

Now she'd handed all that over to Pierre's wife and could sit in her new coral-coloured dress and relax with a pastis. She'd learned not to ask for this outside the villa, as waiters tended to regard it as something only men should drink.

She estimated she had about a quarter of an hour before the musicians arrived and she had to go and settle them in. She fitted a cigarette into her tortoiseshell holder and gave herself up to fifteen minutes of thinking about Patric. It was how she was at the moment. Carving up her days and nights into thinking about Patric times and concentrating-on-what-she-was-doing times. Sometimes the concentration went west. She almost dropped the coffee cake this afternoon.

She wondered where he was. Ireland? Was he thinking about her? She knew it didn't work to will someone to think about you. She'd tried that with Ben, with dismal results. I wish I'd asked Patric to come here. It would have been exciting having him here at the party. With me.

She stood up. When he gets back from Ireland, I'll ask him to come down here. It's ridiculous carrying on like this, sparring and pretending. I'll ask him.

She locked her door and went downstairs to wait for the musicians. Pierre had set up the bar and was polishing glasses. His wife had spread the big white damask cloth and was arranging piles of plates and silver cutlery. Against the stone wall of the house were round tables and chairs.

'I know it's a buffet, but standing up to eat is uncivilized,' Ilona had said. 'And men can't just perch on the wall. Men don't have laps. They need a table.'

Gazing at the lamplit terrace, Paula realized that the Villa Fleurie was a place that spoke of parties and good times. Not just sunlit soirées round the pool but wintertimes, too. With the mistral wild in the eucalyptus, she could imagine hurrying across the darkened terrace towards the double french windows of the salon, the champagne-coloured silk curtains left undrawn, the lights ablaze. And there's the flames leaping in the log fire, there's the welcoming drinks trolley and the sound of the rosewood piano seducing you in . . .

'No, Marie-Laure,' her mother's voice was sharp. 'You are not having a kitten.'

'Oh, but, Maman!'

'Come in the kitchen,' Paula said to the girl. 'I've got some magic biscuits.'

Their voices wafted up to Ilona as she emerged from the demented black-and-red bathroom and slipped into her dress. It was full-length scarlet silk with a double skirt, the top layer gently fluted and the bottom layer, from just above the knee, falling into fine pleats.

She laughed as, on the terrace, Marie-Laure predictably informed her mother that *it wasn't fair.*

Ilona was glad this wasn't going to be the stuffy sort of do she had been obliged to organize at the Schloss. She'd had no friends. She was the outsider Englander, unpopular and resented, especially by Hans's starchy relatives. He taught her German, but they despised her accent and the way she found it hard to remember to put the verb at the end of the sentence.

What riled them most of all, Ilona realized, was that she and Hans had been deliriously in love. They would meet up late morning, after Ilona had given instructions to the cook and head gardener. Often they played tennis. Ilona had been school champion, but playing against an athletic man sharpened her game even more. Or he would take her for a drive. Ilona tried to learn, but the Mercedes was too heavy for her to manoeuvre, and it never seemed to occur to Hans to get a smaller car.

After lunch, if he didn't have a business meeting they went to bed. Oh, those long, loving afternoons! How she missed them!

'Ilona?' It was Paula calling from the terrace. 'Are you ready?'

Ilona fastened a gold locket round her neck and automatically reached for Hans's watch. She had worn it every day since he died. And then, on a sudden, sure impulse, she placed it back on the bedside table. Tonight, Ilona told herself, was to be timeless.

In Liz's bedroom, Kit had just presented her with a perfect red rose. 'I love you, Lizzie.'

They sat on the bed, shoving the muslin out of the way. Liz touched the rose and felt like dissolving into tears. She'd had an awful few days. They'd bought her a very nice white top, off-the-shoulder thing, and an insultingly huge length of midnight blue taffeta. Just how big do they think I am? Liz thought indignantly. What they hadn't thought to buy was a zip. I suppose they couldn't find anything industrial enough.

Anyway, it meant she'd had to flog round Cannes looking

for a haberdasher. Then, yes, she'd found a Singer sewing machine in the cupboard under the stairs; but no box of cottons. Back to the haberdasher for two reels of midnight-blue Sylko. That meant she'd been obliged to run up the skirt and handstitch the hem this morning, because in the afternoon she had to help Paula with the buffet food.

And now Kit had given her this rose. Told her he loved her.

He looked so handsome. White trousers, white shirt, white linen jacket. She got a grip on herself. 'Now you know what you've got to do?'

He said miserably, 'I've got to kiss her.'

'That's right. And you'd better make a good job of it. Because I shall be watching.'

'You're not wearing Hans's watch.' Paula noticed at once.

'No. Too heavy with this dress. Oh good. They're starting,' as the musicians launched into a swing version of 'Anything Goes'.

It was eight o'clock; just into twilight. People were arriving. Joleen had appointed herself chief greeter, which was just as well because Ilona didn't seem to know anyone except the a cappella group. She noticed Kit chatting to the prettiest girl singer.

Both Paula and Ilona were astounded that Joleen wasn't wearing any jewellery apart from her cocktail watch.

'And Lizzie looks OK,' said Ilona. 'That top works well on her.'

Paula went across to Liz. 'At suppertime, would you help Lady Kilmartin get food from the buffet.'

'Why?' Liz demanded. 'Is she crippled?'

Paula said tightly, 'She may not be used to buffet-style eating.'

'Nonsense. What about those country-house breakfasts, helping yourself to kedgeree?'

'You don't help yourself. There is always someone to serve you.'

'Well, anyway, I don't happen to know who Lady Kilmartin is.'

'I'm sure Joleen will be delighted to tell you.' Surrounded by the laughing throng, Paula felt suddenly alone. She went into the salon and turned on the television. Then flicked it off again as Colin appeared at the door. 'I – I was just watching the news.'

He grinned. 'Do you remember what people did when they first had the goggle-box? We didn't have one at home. Couldn't afford it. But when I went round my mates, what they used to do was switch on the set and then switch off the light. We all sat there watching television in the dark. I wonder why.'

Paula shook off her blues and linked her arm through his. 'Come on. Stiff drink.' At the bar she said to Pierre, 'Have you got any gin and tonic?'

Pierre smiled his devastating smile. He had gin, he had tonic, he had sliced lemon, he had ice.

'Make that two,' said Colin, 'and make mine a double.'

A minute later he raised his glass to Paula. 'Great party.'

'Thanks. Though I don't know what's got into Liz. Talk about bear with sore head. So unlike her.'

'Papa!' Paula repressed a groan as Marie-Laure clung to her father's arm and wheedled, 'I can have a kitten, can't I? Say I can, Papa, please, please, please.'

'Come and sit with me for supper, Colin.' Paula took him by the arm, and Colin selected a table within reach of Pierre.

'I'll just stay on the liquid diet for the moment,' Colin said, relieved that Pierre had packed that whiny child off to its mother.

'Isn't this an adorable house, Colin? I never want to leave.'

I do, he thought. With a million quid in my pocket.

'Business OK, Col?'

She had to be joking. But he just told her stuff that would amuse her, like the way fishfinger burgers had bombed, big time.

On the other side of the terrace Lady Kilmartin wrinkled her nose at Liz. 'Is this salad cream?'

'No. Mayonnaise.'

'I see. That's something, at any rate. And what are the green things in this dish?'

'Olives, Lady Kilmartin.'

'I know what an olive is, child. What I don't understand is why the inside is red.'

'Pimento. It's stuffed with pimento.'

'Indeed! How peculiar.'

'Not really. They're easier to eat with false teeth.'

There was a brief roll of drums. As silence fell, the lead musician announced, 'Now, delicious though the food is, I hope you're not eating too much. Because I want to see you all on the floor. Dancing, that is, not paralytic.'

Under cover of the laughter, Liz excused herself from Lady Kilmartin and went to have a quick word with the bandleader. Kit was just emerging from the house. As per instructions he had run a comb through his hair and held his hands under cold water for a minute.

As Liz passed him she muttered, 'One, two, three – go!'

When the band started to play, Kit walked purposefully across the terrace. Liz saw the eyes of every woman at the party directed at him. I've been like that, she thought. Sitting there, willing someone to come and ask me to dance. Anyone. Let alone a man with Kit's film-star looks.

Kit walked past the expectant a cappella girls, past Paula's table and stopped in front of Ilona. He held out his

125

hand; cool after the soak in cold water. 'May I have the pleasure of this dance?'

Ilona rose. 'A waltz. How lovely. It's "The Tennessee Waltz", isn't it?'

Kit hadn't a clue. He had never in his life dreaded anything so much as the next three minutes. OK, later on he'd got to kiss her, but when you'd bummed round the world as much as he had you were obliged to kiss a lot of strange women, in a lot of strange places. No need to go into all that with Liz of course.

Oh Christ. Everyone was staring at them. Everyone.

Ilona said, 'Kit, I'm not going to be very good at this. I learned at school, but the teacher always made me be the boy. And Hans hated dancing. He was hopeless.'

Kit was beginning to warm to Hans. He took Ilona firmly in his arms. 'Don't worry. Just hold on to me.'

No one could take their eyes off the man in white dancing with the woman in the floaty scarlet dress. They looked sensational.

'You're a wonderful dancer,' Ilona smiled. 'Don't tell me it's something else you learned in the Navy?'

He wished she'd shut up. In his head, over the haunting melody of 'The Tennessee Waltz', Kit was tuned in to the soft-baked-biscuit voice of Victor Silvester. 'Right side, together. Left side, together.'

Oh bloody hell. They were approaching a clutch of guests sitting on gilt chairs. This constituted what Kit most wanted to run away from. A corner.

A corner meant you couldn't just stop, shuffle round and start again. It meant he had to guide Ilona through a quarter-turn. God, the laughs he and Lizzie had had, trying to get this right, tripping over the television flex and tipping poor old Victor off the Dansette.

It was OK. With Victor's famous footprint chart flashing through his mind, Kit got his partner round the corner and was just wondering how much longer it was all going to go on, when to his despair the bandleader began to sing:

> I was waltzing with my darlin' to the Tennessee Waltz
> When an old friend I happened to see
> Introduced her to my loved one and while they
> were waltzing
> My friend stole my sweetheart from me.

'I'm very surprised,' Lady Kilmartin said to Liz, 'to see that gel dancing. And wearing a red dress.'

Liz could hardly speak. She'd simply asked the band-leader to play a waltz. Something Kit could dance to. How was she to know they'd play this waltz, with these words?

> I remember the night and the Tennessee Waltz
> Now I know just how much I have lost
> Yes, I lost my little darlin' the night they were playing
> The beautiful Tennessee Waltz.

'Such bad form. I hear her husband only passed on a few months ago.'

Liz made an effort. 'But he was ill, dying really, for years. She'd have done her grieving then.'

Lady Kilmartin looked unconvinced. Liz struggled on, 'To be quite honest, I think what she's feeling now is love-less.'

Mercy be. It was over. Kit whirled Ilona round, she gave a graceful curtsy and everyone applauded.

Liz just wanted to rush up to them, shove Ilona out of the way and kiss Kit. Instead, she said to Lady Kilmartin, 'And, let's face it, if someone like him asked you to dance, would you say no?'

After a stunned few seconds, Her Ladyship lit into a

smile. Watching Kit lead Ilona to the bar for a fruit juice, she said, 'No. I must confess. I wouldn't say no.'

Joleen bustled up, taffeta petticoat all a-rustle.

'Lady Kilmartin, may I fetch you some coffee cake?'

'I've already had some, thank you.'

Joleen smiled regally at Liz. 'Thank you, Lizzie. I'll look after Lady Kilmartin now.'

As Liz made her escape, Lady Kilmartin said, 'What a bonny girl.'

Joleen sat down. Bonny meant fat. 'Poor Lizzie. We all feel so sorry for her. No hope of a husband, of course.'

'Is there any money?'

Joleen shook her head.

'Oh well,' shrugged Lady Kilmartin, 'then she's doomed.'

Joleen was waving at Ilona, hoping she'd come across. 'Don't you think she looks like Princess Grace?'

'Well, that one was no better than she ought to be. None of her leading men were safe, so I hear. But what do you expect? Daughter of a builder.'

The dance area of the terrace was packed. Joleen waved at Colin, still sitting near the bar. He waved back. She waved more frantically. She wanted him to come and ask Lady Kilmartin to dance. Or at least come and talk to the old bat.

Lady Kilmartin touched Joleen's arm. 'My dear. Unless one is royal, one does not wave. It's common.'

Joleen resisted the urge to seize the rest of the coffee cake and smash it into Lady Kilmartin's face. Instead, she went across to Pierre. 'Vodka tonic, please. Large.'

Colin cut in. 'Take it easy, Joleen.'

She ignored him. Smiled winningly at Pierre. 'Are you allowed a little break? We could have a little dance.'

'Sorry,' he said. 'I have to stay here.'

'You've got a wonderful smile.'

Colin grabbed her and dragged her away.

'Hey! I haven't had my drink. I haven't had my vodka!'

'For God's sake, Joleen. Try and show some class.'

'And just who are you, Colin Love?' Joleen exploded. 'I may have been trailer trash, but you were just an out-of-work jerk. You'd be nothing without me,' she shouted. 'Nothing!'

It was, Colin realized, turning into a right bad party.

Down by the deserted pool Ilona was undressing.

'That's a lovely dress,' Kit said, thinking, Hell, she's going to do her swimming-naked act. They'd all seen this performance every morning. And, yes, they all knew she was a natural blonde.

'Coming in, Kit?'

'I'd rather watch you.'

Liz had put a firm kybosh on buff swimming. 'No, Kit. You know what happens to men in cold water.'

What struck him was that when Ilona dived naked into the pool in the morning she could convince herself that no one at the house was yet up to see her. Tonight, however, the show was clearly exclusively for him.

And some show. Ilona had forsaken her usual back-stroke pyrotechnics. She just lay on her back, floating. Her arms were spread, her legs were spread, her eyes never left his face.

For something to do he picked up her dress and laid it with deliberate reverence over a deckchair. As he did so he noticed that the pool boy had forgotten to put out towels. By the time Ilona climbed out of the water Kit knew what to do. He gave her his handkerchief so she could dry off enough to put on the red silk panties. Then he took off his jacket and unbuttoned his shirt. 'Here, put this on until you get dry.'

Laughing, she shrugged on the white linen shirt. Kit had to admit she looked absolutely terrific.

He put his jacket back on and said, 'Will you run away with me?'

'Sure. How far do you want to go?'

'Well, the beach would be a good start.'

Kit opened the garden gate. It smelled of creosote, which to Kit would always remind him of childhood summers, playing cricket with Hugh in the days when he'd been Hughie.

Come on, he told himself. Eye on ball.

As they took the path that led to the sea, Kit reflected that it would have been much easier if they could have gone to the pictures. Something where Cary Grant could do a bit of spade work for him. While the girl was glued to the screen, he could move in with the arm-round routine. Test the water a bit.

The sea was lustrous under the full moon. It was a night just made for romance. Kit led Ilona to the spot selected by Liz and murmured, 'Sit down.'

'Don't say "shall we" or "would you like to",' Liz had said. 'Be masterful. Give commands. Women like that.'

As Ilona sank on to the sand he saw she was, slightly nervously, fingering her locket. Don't ask, thought Kit. Don't ask what's in that locket. It's bound to be a picture of Hans or a slice of his bloody hair. Besides, Kit had a more urgent problem. Which side of Ilona to sit. Liz had said she would be watching, but he didn't know where from. He wanted her to have a good view. Even Liz had to admit he was a fantastic kisser.

'Strewth, he could hear Ilona breathing, see the rise and fall of her breasts in the white shirt. And, Christ, the heat coming from her. Just to make sure, he brushed his hand up the back of her neck. Her reaction was immediate.

Sharp intake of breath. Head falling back. Mouth moist, soft . . .

Don't rush it, he ordered himself. Remember The Plan.

This is your future bride, and this is our first kiss. Something she's supposed to remember for ever.

He gazed at her intently, hoping the moonlight was bright enough for the smokies to have effect. Gently but firmly he took her face in his hands. She was trembling.

Take your time. Keep control.

She looked ready to faint. He gave a slight sigh, as if to indicate an infinite yearning. And then, at last, he gave her the kind of kiss she wanted.

Up on the road bridge Liz felt she should be applauding. The hands-round-the-face bit had been her idea, and they'd enjoyed themselves rehearsing it. Oh, he was doing well.

Too well. She'd schemed and planned and plotted to get that embrace under way, but she'd been so concerned about getting Kit out of Sharkey's clutches she'd suppressed the most natural emotion in the world.

Jealousy. She felt swamped with jealousy. Sick with jealousy. Leave him alone, she wanted to scream. He's mine! Leave him alone!

But Ilona clearly had no intention of letting Kit go. Liz watched in horror as the woman in the white shirt and red knickers pulled her boyfriend down on top of her on the sand. The bitch! She's got his jacket off. She's got him lying down. And they were kissing and kissing and kissing.

In a frenzy of angst-ridden panic Liz wondered if she should rush up – jolly old Liz – and start chattering on about something. Anything.

No. Wrong. To stay in character Kit would have to tell her to clear off.

He couldn't really be enjoying it, could he? He hadn't been lying all this time, pretending he preferred me when all the time he fancied her. Couldn't wait to get his hands on her . . .

Liz burst into tears. This was torture. It was all her fault, and how did you wipe your eyes on a skirt made of taffeta?

Colin was beginning to wonder if anyone was enjoying this blasted party. Joleen had stormed off, Kit and Ilona had simply buggered off, Liz had obviously been crying and that brat Marie-Laure had kicked her mother and got soundly slapped.

The band were playing what was clearly their final number. Colin got a last drink off Pierre before the bar closed and hung around, waiting for the song to end. It always amused him, the speed with which musicians could play the last note, pack up their instruments and vamoose.

> Good night, sweetheart,
> Tho' I'm not beside you,
> Good night, sweetheart,
> Still my love will guide you
> Dreams enfold you
> In each one I'll hold you,
> Good night, sweetheart, good night.

And that was it. Bang! They were gone.

Colin fetched himself a cold chicken leg and salad. He lurched off to find Liz. She wasn't in the kitchen or the salon. He hoped she hadn't gone to bed. Then he saw there was a light on in Patric's library. Liz was on the daybed, hugging a velvet cushion.

'You OK, Lizzie?' He sat down next to her.

'Hunky-dory.' She nodded towards his plate. 'Tell me what you think of the mayonnaise. I made it. Paula showed me. She was amazing this afternoon. She'd made coffee cake, but when she came to get it out of the fridge she knocked it and a bit dropped off and then Constanza trod on it. And Paula said, "Oh, never mind, I'll just whip up some more sponge mixture and we'll stick some icing over the lot." So cool. I would have freaked.'

Listening to her rambling frantically on, Colin wanted to hug her. Actually he wanted to finish his chicken and then hug her. He should have asked her to dance. Poor thing, sitting there like a wallflower all evening.

'Tell you something, Liz. This mayonnaise is very nice. But I'd really prefer salad cream.'

It was good to see her smile. She had a lovely smile. And those knockers were something else. He shoved his plate on to a side table, took the velvet cushion away from Liz and put his arms round her. 'You know, Lizzie, I've got a real thing about you.'

She said gently, 'Colin, you're plastered.'

'I know. Doesn't stop me wanting you, though.'

Liz had just thought, Oh why not? when Kit walked in. She saw he had got his shirt back and was sliding his car keys into his jacket pocket.

'Er, I'm just waiting for Ilona to get changed. She wants me to take her for a drive.'

Liz gave him a look that said 'over my dead body'. Then Paula appeared and asked Colin, 'Where's Joleen?'

He shrugged. 'Why?'

'Lady Kilmartin wants to say goodbye to her.'

'Isn't it usual to say goodbye to your hostess? Joleen is just a guest.'

'Yes, but Lady K thinks she might have said something to upset Joleen . . .'

Colin guffawed. 'Not difficult, is it?'

'. . . And she wants to smooth things over. The chauffeur's arrived, but I can't find Joleen.'

'I saw her earlier near the pool,' said Liz. 'She won't be difficult to spot. She's wearing Ilona's red dress.'

Paula left. Colin fell off the daybed and staggered after her.

'Christ, all this coming and going,' said Kit. 'It's like one of those farces called *When Did You Last See Your Trousers?*' Then, responding to Liz's look of heaving resentment, 'OK. I admit she's hot stuff.'

'You didn't . . .'

''Course not.'

'But you wanted to. I saw the way you were kissing her.'

'I was doing what you fucking told me! And what about you and Colin?'

'Don't be daft. He would have passed out. You'd better go and see if he's OK. And just to make things clear, you are *not* taking Ilona for a drive.'

Kit found Colin in the hall. He was slumped on the gilt chair next to the phone, trying unsuccessfully to dial. 'Got to get through to the boat, Kit. See if Joleen's gone there.'

The number was on the contact sheet on the phone table. Kit dialled and was put through to the skipper.

'Knut, is Mrs Love aboard?'

'No, sir. I understood she was with Mr Love.'

'Thank you.' He shook his head at Colin.

Colin dragged himself up and started scrabbling in the table drawer. 'Keys. Patric's car. Got to go.'

'I'll drive you,' Kit said.

Five minutes later, with a weary spurt of energy, he was gunning the Daimler down the drive. He was beginning to see this entire evening as some sort of Greek drama, a series of trials over which he, cast as reluctant hero, was supposed to triumph.

'What's this all about, Colin?'

'I think,' Colin began, 'No, I know. I *know* my wife has been kidnapped.'

*

'Where are we going?' demanded Kit. Not the cop shop, obviously.

'Antibes.' And Colin told him about his morning there, searching for Skip's boat.

'Skip ran my first yacht. Joleen never liked him. I must admit he was a helluva rogue. And that's just what I was looking for in Antibes. A rogue . . .'

'I had a feeling you'd turn up,' Skip had said.

'Can we go below?' Colin had asked.

By the time they'd finished their beers Skip was saying, 'I don't see why you can't just ask this Ilona to help you out. What's a million to her? She must be worth fifty times that.'

'I can't run the risk of her telling Joleen. My wife must never know how seriously on the skids we are.'

Skip had opened two more beers.

'OK. Recap. No violence. No, no. I wouldn't want her hurt.'

'Always your undoing, Col. Never knew how to treat a woman rough. Take that wife of yours. If you'd slapped her arse a bit, she'd have reined in the wild spending and you wouldn't be in this shit.'

Colin had forced him to keep to the point. The villa party. Ilona easy to recognize in a red dress. 'When you get to the villa –'

'Correction. I don't do the heavy stuff myself. There's two guys I know who work as a team on this kind of job. They nab her, and between us we convey her to a place of safety.'

'Where?'

'Over the border. I'll work out the details. Best you don't know. And after today you don't know me.'

Colin had asked about the ransom note. The money.

'Won't be a ransom note. That's crude, and it's evidence. Ilona will be contacted by one of my guys experienced in this sort of negotiation. If things drag on or she proves tricky, he'll contact you, and I advise you to haul in someone on an equal footing with him to help negotiate. It's no good you doing it. You'd be in such a state you'd screw up.'

The money, Colin had repeated. How would he get the money?

'She will arrange a transfer of one million quid in cash to a numbered account in Zurich. My guy will remove the dosh, close his account and bring the cash to Monaco to hand over to you. Happens all the time. Talking of money . . .'

'Oh yeah. Right.'

From his jacket pocket he had brought out one of Joleen's velvet jewellery bags. Skip tipped on to the table a mass of gold bracelets, rings, necklaces and earrings.

He whistled. 'She not gonna miss all this?'

'Nah. This is the stuff she never wears.'

Skip had lit a roll-up. 'Col, are you sure you want to do this? I mean, if you sold your boat, your place in London –'

'Joleen would flip. She grew up poor. The boat, the big house, they mean everything to her. She loves being on a par with Lady Mirabelle This and Rupert Farting Bodkins That. She just loves it.' He stood up. 'I better go, Skip. Oh, these heavies of yours. They're gonna be alone with Ilona, right? I don't want any funny business.'

'Understood, Col.'

THIRTEEN

THE DAY AFTER the party Ilona was the only one at the villa with a clear head. She was sitting on the terrace with her back half turned to Kit. He gathered that his sudden defection last night had not gone down well. Pity. He could still taste her. Hot and sweet, like mulled wine.

Having had a fruitless nightmare time in Antibes, Kit had joined Colin in an unwise glass of cognac before Colin had crashed out on the library daybed. He was still there. The cognac, instead of sending Kit to sleep, had given him a restless night and a head that felt full of shrapnel. At dawn Liz had got into bed with him, and they'd had the Ilona row all over again, only it was worse when you had to shout in whispers.

Now she was preparing a late breakfast, setting out croissants, bread and *confiture* on the table under the pergola.

'I feel completely wretched,' Ilona said. 'They were obviously after me. Dear Joleen. What if they've hurt her?'

Constanza, in between clearing up and finishing bottles of wine, had found Joleen's dress, starched petticoat and cocktail watch near the pool and, for some reason, laid them out near the lavender border.

'You'd better phone Patric,' Ilona told Paula. 'Get him here.'

'Why me?' Paula resented her tone. 'Why can't you phone? Anyway. He's off the radar. In Ireland.'

'I know. He always goes at this time of year. You'll have to speak to Mrs Armstrong. She'll know where he is.' Mrs Armstrong was Patric's secretary. Paula had already dealt with her over arrangements for her flight, and her remuneration – '*And I understand, Miss Montgomery, that Mr Ryan will be paying you out of his personal account.*' Like personal services. Like a hooker.

'Ilona, why can't you speak to Mrs Armstrong?'

Ilona shook her blonde hair, still damp from her swim. 'She petrifies me. You're used to difficult clients. She won't browbeat you.'

'It's Saturday. She won't be at work.'

'I have her home number. Patric gave it to me for emergencies.'

As a grim Paula went off to telephone, Liz reflected that it was interesting how calling the police was not an option any of them favoured. Ilona had screamed at the prospect of publicity, of photographers at the gate. Over the gate. The French press were bold and unscrupulous. If they got wind of the story her picture – all their pictures – would be everywhere. She couldn't bear it.

Neither could Kit. Hugh and Annabel might read it. They might decide to exhibit family solidarity and turn up, here at the villa.

Liz, of course, wanted no police snooping around. Life was complicated enough, and who knows what they might unravel.

And Paula had sided with Ilona. She returned from the phone. Kit lit an Olivier and passed it to her.

'That woman!' Paula turned her voice Arctic. '"*Mr Ryan is a very busy man, Miss Montgomery. I wouldn't dream of disturbing him on his holiday.*" "We have a serious crisis here at the villa, Mrs Armstrong. I think Mr Ryan would be extremely displeased if he wasn't informed." "*Indeed! What exactly has occurred?*"

Paula had felt like saying, she informed the group at the table, 'Look, if your boss wants you to know, I'm sure he'll be the first to tell you.' But, instead, she gave Mrs Armstrong a concise account of what had happened.

At seven o'clock that evening, the postboy brought a telegram. It was addressed to Paula. 'Hell,' she said. 'It might be a ransom note.'

'Don't be silly,' said Ilona. 'A ransom note would go to Colin.'

'Too right,' Colin said faintly, having finally got up and sobered up. 'Well, open the thing, then.'

Paula read it out. 'RYAN ARRIVING ELEVEN A.M. NICE MONDAY STOP ARMSTRONG.'

'Oh good,' breathed Ilona. 'He'll know what to do.'

On Sunday Kit and Paula elected to pass the time by making cocktails. Liz, getting lunch, could have throttled Kit for doing what they'd agreed he shouldn't – displaying his bar skills. But there he was with the silver cocktail shaker showing Paula how to make an Americano.

'You need Campari, red Martini and a spoonful of gin. The ones we had that time at Eden Roc, I think they used Noilly Prat, and it doesn't taste as good. Gin's the thing. Then you add a very thin slice of lemon and one of orange, and Bob, as they say, is your jolly old uncle.'

Pissed, thought Liz. I'd better hurry lunch up. As often happened in that part of the world, around midday a wind had got up, driving them indoors. They ate in the dining-room, which Ilona disliked for its formality; much cosier eating round the kitchen table. Liz seemed a bit out of sorts. And Kit and Paula, now hitting the red wine, were sloshed and silly. Colin had done the right thing, going back to the boat to have lunch with his skipper. Ilona wished she'd gone with him. Liz, Paula, Kit, the waiting, the not knowing, it was all getting on her nerves.

She went up to her room. Tried to sleep. All she could think of was Joleen, and how it was all her own fault. Patric had been right. She should never have had a party with such a complete lack of security. Not even a dog. And what was going to happen now? When they found out Joleen was Joleen, would they have another go at Ilona? Were they watching the villa? Who was giving them information? Whom could she trust?

And Joleen. What if they'd harmed her? Right now they might be chopping her into bits.

Abruptly, Ilona got up. She wanted a drink.

Ilona had told Paula she had never liked the taste of alcohol, but this wasn't true. When she had first married Hans he had, despite post-war austerity, an excellent cellar which his father had bricked up as the country headed inexorably towards war, following the same instinct that made him move most of the family assets to Switzerland.

She and Hans had both enjoyed a bottle of wine, sometimes two, with lunch and then again at dinner. After a particularly convivial lunch with one of his business colleagues who had a jokey disposition, Hans drove him to the railway station, and before the servants could get into the dining-room and start finishing up the wine Ilona did the job for them. Most of a bottle. Lovely.

Then she wandered outside. She would have liked to pick some flowers for her room, but the head gardener resented what he regarded as her interference.

The dining-room led on to a terrace which in turn led to an elegantly wide flight of stone steps giving on to a garden stiff with red and white blooms. When she'd first seen the steps she'd asked Hans why there was no hand-rail, and he'd said oh no, you can't have one, it would spoil the line.

She knew how much wine she'd had. Knew she must be careful. The servants would be watching. They watched all the time.

Slowly, carefully, she began her descent. One step. Two steps. Head spinning. Three steps, four. Keep looking down. Five, six. Knees a bit trembly. Keep going. Two more. Just two.

Seven, eight. She'd done it! Well done, Ilona. Well done.

Then she tripped and fell into the flowerbed.

When her maid had put her to bed, and they had both agreed for the fifth time that Ilona's shoes must be sent back, the heels were definitely wobbly, Ilona rested until the room stopped going round, and she thought, I'm turning into my mother.

It was always put about on the Isle of Wight that Mrs Dunbar had a delicate constitution, which was why Mr Dunbar took her off so often for sea and mountain air, as a tonic.

The only tonic Ilona's mother felt she needed was the small amount she took in her gin. Mrs Dunbar was a dipsomaniac. A drunk.

And I'm going the same way, thought the newly married Ilona.

She hadn't touched a drink for ten years; kidded Hans that her doctor had told her that alcohol seriously reduced a woman's fertility. Since they were both anxious for a child, he had swallowed her story.

Now, at the villa, Ilona felt again the old craving she'd once feared would over-rule her. It was more than a thirst. It was a burn in the throat, a clawing in the gut, a fist in the back, propelling her across the room and down the marble stairs, and please let it still be there and let there still be booze in it.

It *was* there, on the drinks chariot. The silver cocktail shaker. Half full. Good old Kit. She grabbed the shaker and a glass. Ran back upstairs.

She opened the door to her terrace. The wind had dropped. She poured the Americano and put the glass and the shaker on the small table while she settled herself in her deckchair. Now she'd done it, gone and got herself a drink, she felt in no rush. She could savour this. There was plenty in the silver shaker. And if she wanted to, she could go and make some more. So what?

Slipping a cushion behind her neck, she lifted her face to the sun. It was hot. She'd always been able to take the heat. Always turned browner than anyone else on an Isle of Wight beach. Even Paula, with her olivey skin, she rarely got as bronzed as . . .

'Ilona! Come on. We're going for a swim.'

Groggy with sleep, Ilona heard Paula. She was somewhere in the bedroom.

Ilona opened her eyes. How long had she been asleep?

She got to her feet. Focused. Remembered. Realized that the full glass of Americano had gone. So had the silver cocktail shaker.

So had Paula.

The next morning, with the master of the house expected, activity at the villa was frenzied. From first light Constanza got to work on the place with enough cleaning materials, Paula remarked, to swab out an abattoir.

At least that brought a smile to Colin's face. He looked dreadful but was keeping busy, in the absence of the pool boy, shining the convertible prior to driving to Nice airport to meet Patric.

Ilona had cornered Kit in the salon. She was wearing Hans's watch again, he noticed.

'. . . And another thing, Kit. Patric's a lawyer. He'll want to know exactly what went on at the party.'

Kit smiled. 'I don't know about you, but I rather enjoyed what went on.'

She was fingering her locket. 'I just think – if you don't mind – if you wouldn't –'

'Kiss and tell? One is a gentleman, madam.'

'Oh, there you are, Kit!' Liz bustled in with straw shopping baskets. 'Could you give me a lift to the market?'

'Good idea,' Ilona said. 'With Patric coming, we'd better stock up. Get Paula some pastis.'

In the car Liz confessed. 'I'm dreading meeting this Patric. If she's so in awe of him, he must be terrifying.'

Kit said he gathered that Ilona was expecting Patric to give her a verbal slapping for the lack of security at the party.

Liz snapped, 'You're going the wrong way. The market's in Cannes.'

'We're going to the one in La Bocca,' Kit said. Since he was obviously still in the dog-house, he tried to improve her mood by showing her his discoveries. The lively market, the shops, the café.

And then he took her to La Cachette. Liz looked at the tiled roof, the blue shutters, the lemon tree and the silvery leaves of the olive tree in the garden.

He heard her wistful sigh. 'We'd be OK there, Lizzie. I could get work on the boats, crewing. We could grow our own veg.'

They were sitting on the grass bank. He had hold of her.

'We don't need to do this Ilona thing. As soon as we know Joleen is safe we could jump ship. Sharkey would never find us here. No one's ever heard of La Bocca. Especially those shits in Streatham. We could come here and just be us.' He kissed her. 'I've missed us, Lizzie.'

'I know. I know. I've missed us, too. But it takes a woman to know a woman. And it's all gone too far, Kit. I can tell you, she won't let you go. Not now.'

She turned her back on La Cachette, and they returned to the car.

'Awful for Colin,' Liz said. 'That shrew of a wife, and no money.'

They discussed the bizarre scenario where Colin might have to pay a million quid ransom – money he didn't have – to get back a wife he didn't want. They also agreed not to tell Ilona and Paula that Colin was skint. Colin was adamant Joleen was not to know, and the girls might spill the beans when Joleen got back.

If she got back.

At the villa Paula was out, and Ilona was arranging a jug of the pretty blue plumbago to decorate the damask luncheon cloth. She was wearing a white pleated dress, and as Patric's car appeared she ran down the drive to greet him. Liz washed her hands and waited at the bottom of the stairs.

Paula was loitering in Cannes, trying to summon the courage to walk into the villa and say hello to the man who didn't know she'd fallen in love with him. She downed a pastis, braving the disapproval of the waiter, and then made herself retrace her steps to the villa. As she entered the cool of the hall Liz came out of the kitchen.

'Any news, Lizzie?'

''Fraid not. But Mr Ryan is here.'

'Yes, I saw his car.'

Liz smiled her most demure smile. 'The thing is, I asked Ilona where I should put him, you know, and she said he'd probably be best in with you. So that's where he is now.'

Ilona had said no such thing. What she had said was that it was a bit complicated and that Patric and Paula would have to sort it out themselves.

Paula said, 'I locked my door when I went out.'

'Yes. But it is his house. Naturally, Mr Ryan has a key.'

Liz returned to the kitchen, delighted with herself. With Paula keeping Patric occupied at nights, the less chance there was of him roaming about the house and hearing her and Kit.

As soon as the kitchen door closed, Paula took the stairs two at a time. On the landing she paused, trying to compose herself. Her heart was thudding. He was here. He was in her room. Their room. Oh God.

She opened the door and just stood there. Don't run to him. Make him come to you.

The dark-haired man was sitting at the bureau. He saw her and stood up. He wasn't smiling. The blue eyes were regarding her coldly. 'I have an apology to make to you.' She saw he was holding her loose-leaf folder. 'I thought it was a work folder. I was curious – how you were getting along with your book. I didn't realize there would be anything personal in here. I'm sorry.'

His tone was icy. It was the sort of professional apology, Paula thought, a barrister would make in court. The judge, the jury, everyone in the place would know he didn't mean it but honour would be satisfied.

She felt the life draining from her. Hell, she could see where this was going. Frantic, she tried to retrieve the situation, get back to a state of warmth with this man.

'I kept your poem in there. The one you sent me.'

His face softened slightly. But his voice was still cutting.

'I'm glad you liked it. You evidently also liked this.' He flung on to the bed a photograph. It was Hans, on his wedding day, a gardenia in his lapel. 'You tore up a picture of your boyfriend –'

'Ex-boyfriend.'

'But you kept this one of Hans. You still haven't forgiven Ilona for making off with him, have you? If he was still alive today you'd be scheming to get him off her.'

'No! It's not like that. I just kept the photo because I like to have keepsakes of my friends.'

'Yes? And where is your souvenir of your good friend Ilona? This is her wedding picture. A rather special event in her life. But she's not here. You cut her off it.'

'I didn't! It was sent to me like that. Ilona doesn't like having her photo taken. She says she always looks awful.'

'Really? Ilona? Awful? May I suggest that you study the photograph of Hans and Ilona's wedding on the piano downstairs. They are both in the picture. Ilona, as you might expect, looks radiant.'

He closed his attaché case and picked up a worn leather overnight bag.

Paula said, 'Where are you going?'

'I'll base myself in the library.'

'But this is your room.'

'Not with you in it.'

'We can share.' How bad was this? Paula couldn't believe herself. Begging.

'Sure. How seductive, lying with a woman who's dreaming of another man.'

'I don't!' He was nearly at the door. 'Look, *I'll* move to the library.'

'I think it would be best, once we've sorted out getting Joleen back, for you to move yourself back to London.'

And Patric Ryan went downstairs.

*

The atmosphere over lunch was doom-laden. Patric had said he wanted to talk to them individually to try to get some clues as to what happened that night. He had, of course, heard Colin's story in the car coming from the airport. Colin and Patric were the only ones eating. Everyone else felt as if they were waiting to be called to the headmaster's study.

Paula was summoned first. Patric sat at his desk in the library. Briskly, he said he needed a list of everyone at the party. Equally crisply, Paula pointed out that this was difficult. Joleen had done most of the inviting.

'So you didn't know most of the people there?'

'I knew the a cappella singers, and I'd worked for Lady Kilmartin in London.'

'What about the staff?'

'The barman and his wife were recommended by Constanza. I found the band when they were playing at the Martinez Hotel.'

'Right. I want you to go and talk to the band, the a cappella singers – they'll be on the Croisette – and Lady Kilmartin. Just ask if they saw anything unusual, any suspicious characters. I mean, I've never met Joleen, but from what I've heard she wouldn't have gone without a fight.'

Paula laughed. Perhaps now he'd –

'What are you waiting for, Paula?'

'I don't know where Lady Kilmartin is staying.'

'She'll be at the Carlton. Holding court. Take my car.'

Paula flared. 'Why do I have to do this? Why can't you? You're the lawyer. You're used to asking questions.'

'You're doing it because I'm *paying* you to do it.'

The way he underlined that she was no more than an employee, the hired help, inflamed Paula. She couldn't believe this was the same man who'd made love to her, in so many different ways, down the phone.

She couldn't believe she'd let him.

*

147

At the lunch table Ilona took one look at Paula's set face and groaned. 'Bad?'

'Bad. He wants you next. Good luck.'

As Ilona had predicted, she was given a roasting for having the party in the first place, letting Joleen invite half of Cannes and arranging absolutely no security.

Ilona twisted Hans's watch round and round her wrist. There was nothing she could say. It was Patric's villa. His home. One of his homes. He would expect her to look after it.

Then he got on to her movements at the party. 'The dress. Describe it.'

She told him it was red silk with a double skirt, pleated, very fine pleats from the knee and a plainer skirt from the waist, fluting round her hips.

She watched him making notes. Really, the way this interrogation was going, in a minute he'll produce my red dress as Exhibit A.

'So you swam. Then what?'

'I got out of the water.'

He ignored her sarcasm. 'Why didn't you put the red dress back on?'

'I was wet. I – I went back to the house to get changed.' She could not possibly tell him she was wearing Kit's white shirt and very little else. Must remember to tell Kit. Must keep our story straight.

'And then?'

'I went for a walk on the beach.'

'Unescorted?'

'No.'

'Who came with you?'

'None of your business.'

'It *is* my damned business. I'm your lawyer. I promised Hans I would protect you. Now I find you've invited all sorts of riff-raff to this bloody party and gone running off up the beach with one of them. I'm just trying to find out what went on that night. What happened to Joleen.'

'All you need to know,' Ilona fired back, 'is that I wasn't there. I swam. I went to the beach. I came back. I went to change my dress –'

'Another dress?'

Damn. 'I – wasn't happy in the second dress.'

'Didn't you go looking for the first dress? The red dress.'

Ilona wanted to hit him. 'I thought it might be crushed.'

Patric looked at her for a full and, to Ilona, very long thirty seconds. Then he said, 'Oh, go away.'

Liz wiped her clammy hands on her dress and entered the library.

Patric stood up. 'Come and sit down, Liz, and tell me how you met Ilona.'

Liz hadn't expected this. She sank into the proferred chair and tried to keep him on a line of questioning about the party. 'Goodness, it all seems so long ago. Specially with all that's happened. Poor Joleen . . .'

He said patiently, 'Try to remember how you met Ilona.'

She told him how she was on holiday and happened to be in the local shop when Ilona came in for bread. She told him about her bread and cheese, and Ilona raving about the cheese, and driving Ilona to the English shop. She wished he'd stop looking at her like that.

Like he knew.

He turned to a new page in his notebook. 'The party. You're a key person here. You were the one who spotted that Joleen was wearing the red dress. Where were you?'

She told him, thinking, Oh, thanks, I was coming back from one of the worst events of my life, watching the man I love practically devouring another woman.

149

'What did you think when you saw her wearing the red dress?'

'Nothing much.' Think? I could hardly see the dress. My eyes were full of tears.

'What did you do then?'

'I got some food.' A lot of it. Potato salad, apple charlotte, cake. 'I came in here. Then Colin came in with his supper.'

'How did he seem? I mean, calm – excited?'

'He was drunk. It was a *party*, Mr Ryan.'

Liz spotted Kit and Ilona down near the pool. They seemed to be having another of their urgent conversations. It was annoying enough, but particularly when she wanted to tell Kit that things weren't working out with Paula and Patric. Liz had noticed his leather bag near the library daybed. And Paula was in a foul mood. Slammed the door of Patric's convertible and roared off.

She went up to Ilona and Kit, who stopped talking when they saw her. Liz just said to Kit, 'It's your turn', and saw Ilona give his arm a little squeeze. Then Ilona and Kit walked up to the villa together.

It's as if I don't exist as far as she's concerned, thought Liz. Admittedly, she doesn't know about me and Kit. Her thoughts ran wildly on. But suppose it all came out that Kit and I are lovers and this is where we live, at La Cachette in La Bocca. Then what? I'll tell you what. She'd be round, tapping on the window, climbing down the fucking chimney.

'Sorry about all this, Kit,' Patric said. 'It's just we don't want the police involved at this stage, and I need to get a clear picture of what went on.'

'Absolutely,' Kit said, his mind whirring with Ilona's

whispered instructions about the beach, his shirt, her dress . . .

'I understand you had a nightmare time in Antibes with Colin.'

To Kit's relief, that seemed to be all Patric wanted to know. Kit took him through it, stumbling round the darkened quay looking for Skip's boat, Colin refusing to go to the harbourmaster. In the end Kit had gone himself to the *capitainerie* and been told that *Skip's Tub* had left the harbour. But they had no information regarding her destination. Or who was aboard.

'Thanks, Kit. Ask Colin if I could have a word.'

Patric started his chat with Colin by saying he was speaking confidentially. 'Normally, I wouldn't discuss a client's affairs, but this is a special case. However, I don't want you to say a word outside this room.'

'Got it,' said Colin.

Patric leaned forward. 'The point is, this scheme you've owned up to would never have worked. You couldn't have got a million off Ilona. She hasn't got a million.'

Colin laughed. 'Come off it, Patric.'

'She has a very generous monthly allowance from a trust fund set up by her late husband and administered by me. In time, she will of course be worth a fortune. I should think she'll be one of the richest women in the world. But Hans's estate is very complicated. It's going to take a good two years to get it to probate. He had companies all over the world. Different rules, different priorities. The Italians in particular have been driving me up the wall.'

Colin nodded. 'Bloody wops.' Obviously Hans had the trust fund set up to ward off fortune-hunters. Wise move.

'You're a businessman, Colin. Surely you knew that even if Ilona had got a million in the bank, she couldn't have just arranged a cash transfer down the phone. She would have had to go in person. There would be security checks . . .'

Colin faded him out. It was flattering Patric calling him a businessman, and Colin accepted he'd been good at small-time business, but now it had all got so big, so unwieldy, he felt overwhelmed. Everyone blamed Joleen, her extra-vagance, but Colin knew that in truth, when they'd started the business it was Joleen who'd been the driving force. He'd worked hard, God knows, but basically he'd just done what she told him. And it had worked. So as soon as they'd made a pile she backed off and started doing what she'd always wanted to do – buy things. Colin was left on his own to run the show. And even with sound people to advise him, like Ronald C. Beck, he hadn't been able to make a go of it.

Patric was waiting.

'You see, Skip said –' Colin read Patric's face. 'Oh God.'

'Colin, what's Skip's name?'

'I don't know. Just Skip.'

'But he was your employee. You paid his wages.'

'Cash. He only took cash.'

'OK. You gave him your wife's jewellery.'

'Some of it. Not all.'

'What was that worth?'

Colin thought. 'About £50,000.'

'So when Skip finds out they kidnapped the wrong woman, what's he going to do?'

'He's gonna do a runner.'

'Exactly. What worries me is what the heavies might do. Especially if he hasn't paid them yet.'

Patric threw down his pen. 'Let's face it, Colin, you've lost control of the situation. I suspected as much from what you told me in the car. That's why I've had to talk to everyone. Get some clues. But the paramount thing is we have *got* to find Joleen.'

*

In Cannes, as she expected, Paula found the jazz musicians enjoying a late lunch at a restaurant just across the road from the Martinez Hotel. It was a cheery place, frequented by chauffeurs and the girls who 'worked' at the big hotels. There was music on the gramophone, and people were dancing.

The musicians insisted Paula sit down with them. She felt she should be seeking out the a cappella singers, but the jazzmen said they'd gone on a trip to the Var, so Paula relaxed and ordered a pastis.

The jazz guys loved this. If you like that, they said, why not try absinthe? They told her how Oscar Wilde was once chucking down absinthe and saw tulips sprouting from the floor. He said, 'After the first glass, you see things as you wish they were. After the second, as they are not. Finally you see things as they really are, and that is the most horrible thing in the world.'

Paula was only allowing herself the one, but already she felt as if she'd had three. It was just sinking in. Not only that Patric no longer wanted her – he'd fired her as well. Notice to quit. Another man who blew hot and cold. All over you one minute, and you believe him, and you think, Oh, he really does care for me. And then, with this type of man, he's scared he's said too much, scared of what he's feeling. So he slams shut the emotional door and makes sure you don't see him again.

The musicians said they'd seen nothing amiss at the party. Nothing they weren't used to. People drunk, falling over, shouting. The usual.

Paula was longing for another pastis, but two was always a mistake, and anyway she was driving Patric's car. If she had a prang he would probably self-combust.

It was five o'clock when the restaurant party broke up. She walked the short distance to the Carlton Hotel and reluctantly approached Lady Kilmartin on the terrace.

Her Ladyship was wearing a brick-coloured dress with a matching jacket edged in gold braid. Given her rounded proportions, the outfit put Paula in mind of the Queen's orb.

Her Ladyship was drinking a champagne cocktail and, as Patric had predicted, holding court. But to a flock of pigeons.

'Excuse me, Lady Kilmartin. I'm Paula Montgomery.'

Lady Kilmartin peered at her. 'Do I know you?'

Listen, lady, this is 1959, Paula wanted to snap. No one says, 'Do I know you, or who are you?' any more. They say, 'What do you do?'

'I had the pleasure of arranging a cocktail party for you in London.'

'Oh yes,' Her Ladyship said dismissively. 'You're the cook. Well, if you're looking for work, I really don't . . .' She flapped away yet another pigeon. 'Wretched birds. These waiters. So stupid, bringing crisps.'

'I saw you at the party at the Villa Fleurie the other night, Lady Kilmartin, and I wondered if you'd noticed anything unusual or suspicious. You see, one of the girls lost rather a valuable bracelet.'

'No I didn't. All I remember was that new widow. Dancing. In a red dress.'

'You didn't see anyone else wearing the dress?'

'Anyone else! Why would people be exchanging their clothes?' She gave a genteel shudder and said, 'Now run along, will you? I'm expecting some people.'

That's that, then, thought Paula, beating it. And the old trout didn't even ask me to sit down.

She drove back along the Croisette, vibrant with palms, umbrella pines and cactus. The sky and the sea were the same entrancing blue. I'm going to miss all this, she thought. The prospect of returning to the grey skies of London was depressing. Even the Cannes traffic jam had a glamour, with good-humoured holiday-makers showing off exotic Italian cars and girls who looked like film stars, but who probably weren't, dashing across the road on gold high heels, swinging matching gold hand-bags.

It was around six when she parked the car at the Villa Fleurie. She could see the others sharing a bottle of wine at the terrace table. No news, then. No ransom demand. Otherwise there would have been more frenzied activity.

Suddenly, her eye was caught by a flash of red. Just beyond the pool. She did a double-take.

Wait. Yes. There it was again.

She ran round the pool, and there, coming towards her, dressed in scarlet, was Marie-Laure.

'The kittens!' wailed the child. 'Where are the kittens?'

'They're – at the animal hospital. Quite safe.'

'Are you sure? The men said they should be drowned.'

'Men? What men?'

'The men playing the game with the lady.'

Paula kneeled down. 'What colour dress was the lady wearing?'

'Red.'

'And the men. Did they speak in French?'

'Some French, some Italian.'

'How do you know?'

'The lady who lives next door to us is Italian. When she shouts at me she shouts in Italian. She says *vaffanculo*. Maman says it's very rude, but it's what the big man shouted at me when I asked if he'd like to see the kittens.'

Paula took her hand and led her up to the terrace. It was useless asking Marie-Laure why she hadn't said anything before. The reply would be, 'No one asked me.'

At the terrace table Paula said to the group, 'I think you should all hear this.'

It wasn't often Marie-Laure was invited to take centre

stage, and she relished her limelight opportunity. When she got to what had been shouted at her in Italian, Patric laughed.

Kit said, 'What's it mean?'

Patric mouthed at him, 'Fuck you.'

Then he turned back to the child. 'Marie-Laure, why did you think the men and the lady were playing a game?'

She burst into shrieking giggles. When she could finally speak, she spluttered, 'Because she'd put her dress over her head, and you could see all her knickers.'

FOURTEEN

MARIE-LAURE WAS wrong, of course, about why Joleen was wearing the red dress in such a novel fashion.

After her row with Colin, the cystitis was flaring again. Joleen fetched a towel from the villa and went to the deserted pool. She slid off her dress, petticoat, underwear and her watch and eased into the water. It was cool. It was bliss on the bit of her that was burning.

She couldn't swim but splashed around the shallow end and felt much better. Unfair to take it out on Colin, she thought. Even though he has drunk far too much. Better go and find him. Make it all all right.

Out of the pool, she realized that all her energetic splashing had soaked her dress and petticoat. But Ilona's red dress was lying there. Dry. She put it on. It was too long, but the silk felt fabulous.

She was just smoothing the double-layered skirt over her hips when they jumped her. Through a rush of fear she was conscious there were two of them. Sensed it, rather than saw, because the way they trapped her was to pull the skirt of the dress up over her head and tie it. She couldn't use her arms, and she couldn't see.

But all her life Joleen had possessed lung power. She drew breath to scream. They were ahead of her. One of them – he felt alarmingly big and strong – held her, and then a hand, quite gently, explored her face over the red silk. When he found her mouth something – a scarf? – was tied round.

Then she heard the piping voice of Marie-Laure. 'Hello! Would you like to see the kittens?'

And the Italian reply.

Both men were holding Joleen tight. She was seething with frustration. Even if she could let out a yell, the brat was so dumb it wouldn't dawn on her that she needed help.

Desperately, Joleen tried kicking out. Hopeless. She couldn't see what she was aiming at. Besides, without shoes she couldn't do much damage.

And then they took her away. She heard the creak of the garden gate, heard a car motor start. She was pushed in, with one of the men holding her. The engine roared. The automobile seemed to be going very fast. She wished she knew more about cars. Couldn't you tell the make from the sound of the engine? Her bare legs felt a leather seat. Stupid, she realized. There were no clues. The car was probably stolen.

It stopped. She was bundled out. She was picked up, carried. She could hear the clinking sound of boat rigging in the breeze.

Oh God, they're going to throw me in! She tried to lash out with her legs, but then someone grabbed hold of them, and she was somewhere else, sitting, and another engine was starting. A boat engine. She recognized that.

Hell, where are they taking me? And why me? No, she knew the answer to that. She and Colin were rich, thank heavens, but other people had far more money. They were the ones you'd target to kidnap.

The red dress. Obviously they were after Ilona. When I tell them I'm not her they'll either let me go or demand the ransom anyway. And Colin and Ilona will pay it.

This train of thought didn't exactly calm Joleen, but it took her mind off not knowing where she was, where she was going or who *they* were.

She hated not being in control. She felt embarrassed about her bare thighs. As if sensing this, one of the men gently laid what felt like a rough towel across her legs.

She had no idea how long the journey took. At first the sea seemed calm, then it got rougher and the boat was bucketing. The one she thought of as the big one kept hold of her.

Finally the engine slowed. Stopped. Joleen was pulled out of what she assumed was the cabin and once again subjected to a fireman's lift. From the sound, there seemed to be a wooden jetty. Then crunching. Shingle? She heard the boat start up again, stuttering a bit.

The big one set her down. Rough underfoot. A dirt road? The scarf round her mouth was untied. Her mouth was too dry to speak, let alone scream. She was being pushed into something. A confined space. What the hell was it? She was on her own. They'd left her! Perhaps she could –

An engine started. They weren't going fast, just fast enough to deter her from trying to throw herself out of whatever this weird vehicle proved to be.

Short journey. One of them – the nice one? – helped her out of whatever it was. She heard the sound of a door being unlocked. She could hear the thump of the sea. She was taken up some stairs, cement or stone under her bare feet.

'You are here,' one of them said, in heavily accented English.

A bright light. Her dress being untied, freeing her arms, covering her legs. She blinked for a bit, and then she could see.

As she'd thought, there was a big one and a small, wiry

one. Both dark, with brown eyes. The small, young one was pouring her a plastic cup of water. As she gulped it down, the big one blocked the door.

'Come. Look.' The small one was showing her round as if it were a plush hotel. He opened the door to a toilet and hand-basin. There was a towel, soap, a comb, a toothbrush and a tin of pink toothpaste. Back in the room he pointed proudly to the lampshade shielding the bulb hanging from the centre of the ceiling. Apart from a table with pieces of bread and a plastic jug of water, the only other item in the place was a wood-framed bed.

Joleen sighed. At least it all looked clean.

The big one, the older one, asked, 'You like? We were told to treat you with respect.'

He beckoned to his companion. They left the room. Locked the door.

Exhaustion ambushed Joleen. She poured more water, turned out the light and fell on the bed.

She was alive.

They didn't seem unkind.

Tomorrow she'd tell them she wasn't Ilona . . .

She awoke with a sense of dread, then remembered where she was and what had happened.

It's so unfair. It should be Ilona, not me. It's all Colin's fault. If he hadn't been so foul to me at the party I wouldn't have wandered off, wouldn't have put the dress on and then I wouldn't be in this mess. It was all Colin's fault.

She switched on the light, went to the bathroom, washed, cleaned her teeth and put the dress back on. As prisons go, she thought, this could be worse. *En suite* facilities, anyway. Now let's inspect the view.

There were two windows. She opened the inside shutters of the one near the bed and found she was looking at petrol-blue sea and white rocks. A lot of large white rocks. She contemplated the alarming drop, her bare feet and shook her head.

She switched off the light and padded across to the other window. Throwing open the shutters, she faced a steep hillside, lush with grass. A beautiful valley, with not a person in sight nor any other dwelling, not even a hut.

Joleen guessed the house she was in was modern, replacing an old cottage. The toilet fittings were new, and the shutters worked. The windows were designed so they would only open four inches. She peered out as far as she could and saw, in the narrow road outside the house, a white scooter with a sidecar.

Her eyes narrowed. So *that* was what they'd brought her here in. But why? Why not another stolen car?

There was a knock at the door. A key turning in a well-oiled lock. The small one came in with a tray of breakfast. As before, the big one blocked the door.

Joleen was ready for them.

'Thank you,' she said grandly to the small one. 'Just put the tray on the table, would you.' She stood in the middle of the modest room and addressed the big one. 'Now, there's something you must understand. This is important. I am not Ilona. I am Joleen.'

He stared at her with a total lack of comprehension.

'You were supposed to kidnap Ilona. But I was wearing her dress. You took the wrong woman.'

The big one cracked out laughing. 'It is not true.'

'It is true! Ilona is English. I'm American. Americano! I'm Joleen, *Joleen!*' she was screaming now and as they effected a rapid exit she carried on screaming as she banged away at the locked door.

As time dragged by she accepted that she would have to change her tactics. Joleen had never believed in fighting a losing battle.

OK. This was bad. But no point in letting it get worse. She had no jewellery to bribe them with. She spoke no Italian and very little French. When I get through this, she swore, Colin and I will hire language tutors. The best. The fastest.

For something to do she kept checking the valley window. If someone appeared, she might be able to attract attention. Hours passed. She judged by the movement of the sun. Yet there was no movement on the grassy hill.

In the bathroom she splashed cold water on to the bit that burned. It was agony looking at that cool sea out there and not being able to go and lie in it.

The door opened. After her outburst they had obviously decided there was no need to knock. The Italians, she remembered, were big on temperament. Perhaps they now regarded her as one of them.

The small one came in with a tray and the big one loomed at the door. 'Eat now,' he said. 'While hot.'

She sat on the bed and the small one placed the tray on her lap. It contained a bowl of spaghetti. She tucked in.

'Is good?' asked the big one.

'*Very* good. Delicious.'

'He make it.'

The small one smiled his shy, proud smile and Joleen thought, Wow, he's cute, and, Oh God, how pathetic is this? Now I'm fancying a seventeen-year-old kidnapper.

She tried a smile on the big one. 'Your English is very good.'

'I learn after the war, from Canadian sailors. They good men. And I speak French and some German.'

Handy, Joleen thought, in your line of work. She turned on her big-eyed admiring look. 'Where am I? Where is this place?'

He grinned. 'Where they will never find you. Until they have paid the ransom.'

'But I'm not rich!'

The small one rushed to grab the tray as Joleen leaped up. 'You must listen to me! Look, I have no jewellery. If I were rich I'd have bracelets, ear-rings, necklaces, rings –'

She broke off. They were all suddenly transfixed by her gold wedding ring. Ironically, it hadn't cost much. She and Col hadn't a bean when they got married. It was the least expensive item she owned and the one she treasured most.

She sat down. Sat on her hand. 'No!'

The big one signalled to the small one to collect up the trays. 'Do not alarm yourself, signora. We are not thieves.'

He turned to go.

'Wait! Please. I need help. From the *farmacia*.'

'You are ill? You don't look ill.' Don't sound ill was what he meant.

'I need sodium citrate.' Thank goodness Colin had drilled it into her. 'It's urgent. It's – it's for something women get.'

They looked horrified.

'Sodium citrate. Please.'

They spoke to one another in rapid Italian, and Joleen gathered they were arguing about who should run the errand.

Finally the big one said, 'He will go tomorrow.'

'No! Today. I must have it today.'

From her window she saw him leave on the scooter with the sidecar.

After he returned, he appeared at the door with his companion and the big one said, 'He says they do not have sodium citrate. They will try to find some. But the signora in the *farmacia*, she says to send you this. She made it. She says it help you if you drink it.'

Joleen took the bottle from him. It contained a cloudy liquid. 'What is it?'

'I don't know.'

Joleen shook the bottle and poured a little into her plastic cup. Sniffed and tasted. It was mild. Quite pleasant. A taste from long ago, from childhood. She smiled. 'It's barley water. Or the Italian version.'

They exchanged blank glances. She drank a cupful and said, 'Would you take me downstairs? If I could lie in the sea I'd feel better.'

The big one laughed. 'You try to swim away.'

They all knew this was impossible with all the rocks in the way. But she said anyway, 'I can't swim.'

'You could wave at a boat. So they know to come get you.'

Joleen said desperately, 'Not if I'm just lying in the water. You could tie my hands.'

The big one looked at her. He said at last, 'OK. I tie your hands good.'

'OK. Thank you. Thank you very much.'

'You can rely on it,' Colin said, 'whoever those guys are, my wife is giving them hell.'

They were inside, gathered round the kitchen table. It was just gone eight thirty. No one had slept much. There had been violent storms overnight, circling round Cannes, and it was still teeming with rain.

They had talked, of course, of nothing else but The Situation. Skip had told Colin that Joleen would be taken over the border. They agreed that, from Skip's point of view, if he was transporting Joleen Genoa was easy to get to. But Genoa was a sprawl, and there were countless tiny Ligurian villages where Joleen could be hidden.

'I mean, she'd give them a hard time anyway,' Colin went on, 'but what with the cystitis and not having any medication . . .'

'The what?' Patric poured more coffee. 'Cyst what?'

'Cystitis,' Paula said coldly. 'It's a bladder complaint. Very painful.'

If she thought she could embarrass Patric, she was wrong.

'How is it treated?'

'Sodium citrate,' Colin said. 'But for some reason in this part of the world it's hard to get hold of. You can order it though.'

Kit let out a whistle. 'Hey, I know it's a long shot – but if she has sent the thugs to get the stuff, we might have a lead.'

'Great,' said Paula. 'You mean we telephone each individual Ligurian *farmacia*. And by Christmas . . .' She shrugged.

Kit took out his cigarette case and saw the look Ilona gave it. Bloody woman. She'd make him give it up.

He lit up and won his bet with himself when she moved to open the window a fraction.

'Each little Liguarian pharmacy doesn't phone each individual supplier,' Kit said. 'There is a central *laboratoire* supplying each large area of Italy.'

'How do you know?' began Ilona. Then, 'Oh yes, you told us, you used to work for a pharmaceutical company.'

Hello, thought Paula. She's been doing what I've been doing. Going over and over everything he's said, everything she knows about him.

Kit took a long drag on his cigarette, thinking back to the Italian he'd been friendly with at medical school. They were both genuinely interested in pharmaceuticals. And the same women, he recalled, avoiding Liz's watchful eye.

She said, 'I suppose International Directory Enquiries could give us the number of the lab. And then . . .'

Patric was pushing back his chair. 'I have a better idea.' He went into the library, leaving the door open. He was putting through an international call. Five minutes later, they heard, 'Mrs Armstrong. Good morning.'

Paula whispered to Ilona. 'She's there! At her desk. It's not eight o'clock yet in London.'

Patric was detailing what he wanted. The name of the central *laboratoire* for Genoa. The name of the managing director. 'Then would you call his secretary and say I shall be telephoning in fifteen minutes and I should be most grateful for ten minutes of his time.'

Paula and Ilona were giggling.

'Don't tell me, along with everything else, the paragon speaks Italian,' said Paula.

'No,' said Ilona, 'When Mrs Armstrong speaks, the whole world speaks English with her.'

Twenty minutes later Mrs Armstrong rang back. She had the information.

'I don't know what we'll run into in Genoa, what finance we'll need. No, I don't mean the ransom money, just enough for emergencies. So as a precaution, Mrs Armstrong, would you get in touch with our banking people in Genoa and say I shall be coming in personally to collect the money. Oh, you've already primed your assistant. Excellent.'

Ilona shook her head. 'It's awesome. I wonder if she ever has to do anything else to get her Christmas bonus.'

They giggled nervously again, and Kit thought, Christ, talk about gallows humour. Joleen might be bound and gagged. Tortured. She might be dead.

Patric was through to Genoa, asking for the managing director.

'It's still early,' Liz said. 'He might not be there.'

'He will,' Ilona said. 'These continentals, they visit their mistresses between seven and eight in the morning and then go straight on to work. Hans told me.'

Liz was in lust for Patric's telephone style. I could take a lot of that, she decided. Having your path eased like that.

'Oh Lord Blenkinsop, Mrs Christopher Rowledge will be telephoning shortly . . .' And down the years she heard the jeers of her schoolmates. But she could dream, couldn't she?

Patric was speaking what sounded like fluent Italian. They couldn't understand a word except *bambina* which cropped up again and again.

'God, I hope he hasn't got the wrong end of the stick,' groaned Ilona. 'He's not going on about contraceptives, is he?'

Finally Patric put the phone down and came back to the kitchen. Constanza had made more coffee.

He told them he'd played on the fact that Italians will do anything for their children and expect others to be equally family-committed. Hence, Patric had invented a teenage daughter who was on a walking holiday with a respectable English aunt and who had failed to make contact for two weeks. Naturally, Patric and his wife were worried sick. Naturally, he loved his girl, his only child, with all his heart.

Naturally, Paula wanted to curl up and die. She knew he was play-acting, but just hearing him say 'wife' and use terms of endearment – it hurt.

No, Patric went on, at this stage he would rather not contact the police. 'I'm sure you know how it is with girls who are wilful, headstrong, proud. As the father, the head of the family, you have to keep a protective eye on them, without appearing to interfere.'

Then Patric got to the cystitis, the need for sodium citrate. 'He's ringing me back. If any *farmacia* has asked for it I think we're on the case.'

He turned to Liz. 'The Genoa lab covers a large area. We need a map. Can you dig one out from the library?'

Colin phoned Knut to put the *Lovebite* crew on standby. Then he went into the library where Liz was sifting through the map drawer. She looked at him, shut the door and put her arms round him.

'It's – everything, isn't it?'

He rested against her. 'The thing is. Patric. Everyone. So terrific. But, Liz, I don't know if I want Joleen back.'

'I know.' Liz held him close. 'But you can't be seen not to want her back. How would it look? Even if you split up later . . .'

All morning they all felt trapped in the house, but it was raining so hard a stroll round the garden was impossible.

At five to twelve Patric said, 'Nearly lunchtime. He won't ring now.'

Suddenly, the phone was ringing. He went into the library to take it. When he returned he said to Colin, 'Tell Knut. It's Genoa.'

'I thought you phone sooner,' the big one said to Skip.

'Does anything bloody work in this country?' Skip demanded. 'First my bloody boat grounded getting out of that sodding cove. Then I found all the phones are smashed up.'

The big one laughed.

'Anyway, I take it everything's going OK.'

The big one looked down the hall, out through the kitchen door at Joleen. She was lying in the water. Her hands were tied. Guido was telling her the secret of his spaghetti sauce. The little fool had even told her his name.

'Funny name she got,' the big one said to Skip.

'Ilona? Yeah. Scotch, I think.'

'No, Joleen. Her name Joleen.'

'You're wrong.'

'I not wrong. She shout it at me. Again, and again.'

Skip's first thought was that for some reason Ilona was pretending to be Joleen.

Then the big one went on, 'Funny eyes she got, too. Yellow. Like animal.'

Skip went cold. He'd seen those eyes glaring at him day after day on the *Lovebite*. Even so, he had to be sure. But he couldn't risk coming down himself to check. Couldn't risk being seen by Joleen. Still, what he had seen often enough was Joleen in a swimsuit . . . 'Listen. If it is Joleen she'll have a scar running down her left shoulder blade. Go and look.'

Joleen was thinking her legs were getting nice and brown. She'd observed Guido admiring them. Then the big one came and spoiled it all, yammering in Italian on and on, and the next thing, she couldn't believe it, Guido murmured, 'Signora, excuse', and sat her up and unzipped her dress. The touch of his fingers thrilled down her spine. She'd have adored it if the big one hadn't been looking on.

The big one turned and ran into the house.

Guido did her dress up.

The big one said to Skip, 'The scar. It is there.'

'Bloody hell,' said Skip.

The *Lovebite* rescue party had a problem. The trouble was, it *wasn't* actually Genoa. The *farmacia* calling for sodium citrate was further down the coast in a tiny village called Moneglia.

Patric said to Colin. 'Would you ask Knut if we could sail past Moneglia, get as close as we can and see what we can see. Try and get a fix on the place. Then we'll probably have to moor at Genoa and pick up a car.'

At four in the morning Colin awoke in his cabin to the aroma of baking bread. The chef was at work early. The smell always reminded Colin of his mother, baking all the bread for the caff.

He remembered, one time after one of the good kickings, she came rushing down the alley. He thought she was coming to comfort him, but instead she shoved into a dustbin his father's demob suit. 'Looks like one side of it was made for your father, and the other side for a completely different man,' she complained. 'I wouldn't even give it to a tinker.'

When he had told Joleen that his mother had never really been very loving, she had said, 'Perhaps she didn't know how. Perhaps no one had shown her any love.'

On the *Lovebite* Colin couldn't get back to sleep. He looked round the cabin for something to read. He'd finished his book, and on Joleen's side of the bed were just happy-ending romances and her collection of etiquette books.

Joleen's march to self-improvement had, early in their relationship, turned into a crusade. He'd never forget that time in Florida. They'd slept in the truck, and in the morning she watched him making a hash of digging into an orange. She rummaged in her bag and brought out a Swiss army knife. 'Allow me to show you, Colin, how to deal with an orange.' Deftly, she sliced off the top and the bottom. Then she made six vertical cuts from top to bottom so it was a simple matter to remove each strip of peel.

Joleen. For the hundredth time he wondered where exactly she was. And how he was going to feel, having her back. And how he was going to get his hands on a million quid to save his business.

At first light he went up on deck. Patric was already there. Kit appeared soon after. 'You've got an amazingly well-stocked bar, Colin.'

Colin saw he was holding a shot glass of clear liquid.

'Have I? I just leave the steward to stock it.'

'He's a good man.' Kit thrust the glass at Colin. 'It's Chinchón Dulce. You don't see it very often. Spanish fishermen knock it back before they go out in the morning.'

'Bit early for me, Kit.'

'Go on,' Patric urged. 'I could do with some Dutch courage myself.'

Colin gulped down the Chinchón. The effect was immediate. 'Christ! It . . . it makes you want to have sex with strange women!'

'Message from the bridge, sir.' The crew member addressed Colin. 'Skipper says Moneglia is just coming into view.'

Knut cut the engine speed. The three men dashed to the rail. Kit had the binoculars.

'No wonder Knut couldn't get in here,' Patric said. 'Just look at those rocks.'

'OK, Joleen.' Kit adjusted the binoculars. 'Where the hell are you?'

'In bed,' Colin said. 'She had so many years of having to get up early, when we got established she swore she'd never see another sunrise. I don't care how brutal those thugs are who've got her. No chance they can turf her out of bed this early.'

Bed? Patric was thinking. What bed? She was probably trussed up and chained to the floor. It was what he was dreading most. Finding that they'd done her in.

Suddenly, with a lack of drama that sent Kit escalating in Patric's estimation of him, Kit handed Colin the binoculars and said quietly, 'I think you should take a look. I think we've found your wife.'

'*Where?*'

Patric felt two lifetimes pass watching Colin fiddling with the lenses.

'Where?'

'To the right. Two o'clock. White house. Right on the sea.'

'I can't see anyone.'

'She was there. Red dress. Her.'

'She's not there now.'

Patric said. 'Was anyone with her?'

'Not that I could see.'

'Probably watching from the house. Probably armed. But it's our only lead. That and the *farmacia*. Let's go!' He paused. 'Oh, with your permission, Colin.'

The underslept Colin had now given up trying to work out who was running his boat or his life. One thing he knew. It just ain't me, he thought. I don't seem to be very good at it all, on my own.

He gave the order for Knut to put about and head for Genoa. Within an hour the *Lovebite II* was moored alongside the main quay. Kit had never been before and regretted not having time to linger in such an interesting city. But they had to push on. They found the bank, where Mrs Armstrong's assistant had arranged for a massive amount of lire to be ready for collection. Then they hired a red Fiat.

Kit drove, Colin beside him with the map, which he soon complained was worse than useless, probably drawn up in the time of Patric's grandfather.

They left the main road, and started a long, winding descent towards the sea. When they reached the bottom, there was only one way to go and after half a mile or so Colin said, 'Just slow down. There's a sign pointing right to a *farmacia*. Do you think we should go and ask there?'

'No,' said Patric. 'Let's find the house. Decide what to do. Sorry about the map. Didn't realize it was so out of date.'

'We'll be OK as long as we keep to the little coast road,' said Kit. 'Can't go . . .' His voice tailed off as he saw what was ahead. He stopped the car. They all jumped out.

They said, in unison, '*Fuck!*'

It was a tunnel. Just wide enough for a horse and cart but too narrow for the Fiat. And there seemed to be no other way of reaching the house Kit had seen from the *Lovebite*.

172

'This must be where she is,' said Colin. 'Perfect hide-away.'

None of them wanted to walk down the tunnel. It was pitch dark, and they had no idea how long it was. Or what they might encounter on the way.

Kit was turning the car round, thinking, Shit, I had a feeling this was all going too well. 'The village must be around the *farmacia*. Let's see what we can find.'

The *farmacia* was shut. It was midday. In the square, under the trees, the old men of Moneglia sat staring at the fountain, where a group of teenage boys had gathered with their Lambrettas.

Patric went across. Produced an eye-watering wad of lira. Minutes later the rescue squad were wobbling down the hill on the scooters, back towards the tunnel.

They were all, in their different ways, feeling nervous about what might lie ahead if it did turn into a rough-house.

It's all very well for the other two, thought Colin. Patric was in the war, and Kit did National Service. I skipped that when I went to the States with Joleen. Terrified ever since that the military police would catch up with me. Bad moment when those cops came rushing up on that Greek beach. Told Joleen later, and, of course, she went wild laughing. 'Colin, Interpol is for big-time criminals, not someone who fell in love and forgot to notify the British authorities.'

Patric. Yes, Patric had served in the air force during the war, but after his basic training he'd been seconded to Intelligence. His forte was brain, not brawn.

Kit had a different problem. He'd always been useful in a scrap, no trouble with that. Difficulty was, Liz would be livid if he came back crocked. 'You can't propose to Ilona with a broken nose and your teeth knocked out. Just watch it!'

At the tunnel entrance Patric waved at the others to brake. 'When we spot the house, we'll stop a way off. Otherwise they'll hear us.'

They drove into the tunnel, turning on the Lambrettas' lights. It was pleasantly cool after the heat of the day. After an age – five minutes, ten? – light glimmered at the end of the tunnel. They slowed; emerged into a verdant valley. And a hundred yards ahead was an isolated white house.

They dismounted. Kit wanted to go home. He wanted Liz.

'Colin, you go round the back. Keep watch and wait,' said Patric. 'Kit and I will take the front door.'

Blimey. This is it, thought Kit, as Colin ambled down the road, looking reassuringly like a tourist. Colin cast a quick, casual glance at the house. No sign of movement. He slipped round the back, inching his way. His mouth was dry. We should have brought knives, he thought. Scissors. Anything.

The back door was wide open, the kitchen protected by vertical fly-paper. His parents had put up strips like that at the caff, so he knew these were fresh, because there were no flies stuck to them yet.

He pushed aside two of the strips and peered in. He saw a table with a yellow oilskin cloth. It was set for four. He saw flowers, wild flowers, in a little jug.

He saw Joleen.

She turned from the stove. 'Hi, Col. Saw you coming.'

At that moment the Royal Air Force and the Royal Navy burst through the front door. It would take a week for their bruised shoulders to stop throbbing. Kit leading, they raced down the hall.

'How do you do?' Joleen said to the red-faced Patric. 'Would you like some lunch? There's enough for four.'

Colin grabbed her. 'Where . . .'

'It's OK. They went yesterday.'

'Did they hurt you?'

'No.'

Patric was breathing heavily. 'There's a phone in the hall, Colin. If it's working.'

'It *is* working,' said Joleen. 'I heard it ring yesterday morning, and not long after they left. Said something about getting the rest of their money.'

'So may I suggest, Colin,' said Patric, 'you call Knut to give him the good news, and ask him to phone the villa.'

While Colin was trying out his smattering of Italian on the operator, Patric said to Joleen, 'Did they tie you at all?'

'A bit.'

As Joleen put a large pan of water on the stove Kit saw she was blushing. Or perhaps she was just hot. It was hot in the kitchen.

Patric said, 'If those guys left yesterday morning, how come you didn't call for help, pronto?'

'I don't speak Italian.'

'You could have –'

'Good grief.' Kit realized he would have to get Joleen off the hook. Patric was relentless. 'Is that red wine?'

'I found it this morning,' Joleen said. 'Along with the fly-paper. Shall we open it?'

'Shall we just!'

Joleen made fusilli with Genovese basil sauce, and while they ate told them what had happened since the men jumped her at the villa.

She didn't tell them everything.

She showed them the room she had been locked in, and then Patric suggested that they get the hell out.

'Not yet,' Joleen said. 'I want to talk to Colin.'

'Oh. Of course,' said Patric.

'Absolutely. We'll – er – we'll take a stroll,' said Kit, aware that apart from the steep hill or the tunnel there was nowhere to walk to.

When they had gone she said, 'We'll do the dishes.'

Colin stared at her. Dishes? *Joleen*?

She was gathering up the plates.

'Yesterday they were going to take me to the main road. Dump me there, so I could hitch. I didn't want to go.'

'Yeah, dangerous, I know. But wasn't it mad to stay here? You couldn't be sure we'd find you.'

'I like it here, Col.'

He watched her fill the enamel bowl with hot water and squeeze in the washing soap. 'Here, I'll wash,' he said.

'No, you dry.'

'I hate drying.'

'So do I.'

'Toss you for it.' They were both laughing. He put his arms around her. 'We haven't been like this for years.'

'I know. That's what I wanted to talk to you about.'

Patric and Kit were sitting under an olive tree. Patric said, 'You know, now this is over we ought to take the girls out one night. How about the casino?'

Kit fumbled for a cigarette. Liz had warned him – 'Given your secret past, keep off the subject of casinos. Safer.'

Hearing the laughter from the kitchen, Patric went on, 'Kit, you've got the look of a man who plays a mean hand of poker.' And he took out a pack of cards.

Ilona, Paula and Liz were on the quay in Cannes to watch the *Lovebite II* sail in. As Joleen, waving so furiously she nearly fell in, descended the gangway, Ilona whispered, 'She's still wearing the red dress. I wonder why.'

'She's cut it,' Liz said. 'Cut it off at the knee.'

'She's ruined it, Ilona.'

'Sod the dress,' Ilona said. 'She's safe.'

FIFTEEN

PAULA WOKE UP feeling ill. She knew what it was. She'd had it before. When you lost someone, when the man you loved rejected you, it was like being slowly poisoned. It seeps into your system.

You try the recommended antidotes. Think of other things. Keep busy. Make new friends. Keep up with your old friends, most of whom are away. Get back in touch with your family, who are away or bewildered at hearing from you after so long. 'We're just the same,' they say. 'Nothing new. We haven't changed.'

But I've changed! He doesn't *want* me.

She flung herself out of bed. 'OK. Let's go and make Patric's day.'

He was in the library. She didn't knock. Just marched in.

'I've decided to go back to London by train. So I'm off to the station to book my ticket. May I borrow the car?'

'I'll drive you.' He reached on the bookcase for his camera.

Wonderful, Paula thought. He's going to record the historic moment when I buy my ticket home.

In the harbour the fishermen were unloading their catches straight into the waiting baskets of the local restaurateurs. The sun was glinting on the masts of the yachts. Patric stopped the car at the foot of the rue St-Antoine, the ancient cobbled street that snaked up to the top of the old town.

'Have you had a proper look at Le Suquet?'

She shook her head. Why had he brought her here? The train station was further on.

'We could have some breakfast on the way.'

'Thanks, but I'm not hungry.'

He ignored her flinty tone. 'When the Duke of Windsor was staying here, when he was Prince of Wales, one day, the servants couldn't find him. They tore about the Croisette combing all the best hotels, but no Edward. Then someone thought of the Old Port. Very unfashionable. But there he was, the future King of England, sitting in the sun outside an ordinary *auberge*, eating sea urchins in aïoli. And he said, "Cannes is like a beautiful woman. Charming, but full of secrets."'

Paula forced a smile. 'What was he drinking with the aïoli?'

It was a steep climb through the hidden alleys and passageways of the old town, and Paula was glad of the drinking fountain at the top. Patric led her towards the eleventh-century tower, which, he said, had been built by the monks to fend off the Saracens.

From the tree-shaded place de la Castre the view across the Bay of Cannes was stunning. Gleaming at the quayside below was the *Lovebite*.

'When the English built their grand villas here they had the lawns relaid every year with English turf. It was brought by boat. Lord Brougham got a million francs out of King Louis-Philippe for a new harbour where the turf boat could dock. I mean, in those days –'

'Look,' Paula cut in. 'There's something I want to say. To clear up.'

'No,' he said. 'There's something *I* want to say. About that photo of Hans. I know you didn't chop Ilona off. I asked her. She said she sent you one without her on it.'

While she was digesting this he posed Paula on the wall, took out his Leica and snapped her against the Bay of Cannes. 'I'm not very good at apologizing, Paula. I lead the sort of life where I have to make sure people do what I say. And at times I over-react. I have a Celtic temper. You'll have to get used to that.'

'What do you mean?'

He sat beside her. Gripped her hands. 'I want to marry you, Paula.'

Paula was glad he was holding on to her. Otherwise she might have tumbled off the wall. She rallied. 'Excuse me. Isn't it customary to construct a sentence which includes the words, *I love you*? Or didn't Mrs Armstrong have time to programme that in?'

He was regarding her in a way she couldn't fathom. But now she had the advantage Paula had no intention of letting go. 'And, Patric Ryan, in this particular circumstance, shouldn't you be kneeling down?'

Then she read it. The message his blue eyes were flashing at her. Something along the lines of: Any more of that and I'll kneel over you in a way that'll embarrass the hell out of you. Right here, right now.

He just said, 'Say yes, Paula. Say you'll marry me. Then we can go and get a stiff drink.'

En route to the bar they made plans. Patric wanted them to be married in September, in London. 'Not Dublin. Did that the first time.'

He wanted Chelsea Town Hall, near his house in Old

Church Street. 'I belong to a club there. They could do the reception.'

Nice change, thought Paula. For once I won't have to cook.

Lunch today, they agreed, would be taken at a portside *auberge*. Bowls of aromatic bouillabaisse and crusty bread.

First, a bar, a seat in the sun, an aperitif. Paula had a pastis. Then she had another. She felt wonderful. 'Do you mind if we don't tell the others just yet? I need to phone my mother.'

'Of course.'

'And . . . and . . .'

He grinned. 'Spit it out.'

'Well, will you have to invite Mrs Armstrong to our wedding?'

'I think we'll find,' Patric said, 'that on the appointed day Mrs Armstrong will prove to be promised elsewhere.'

Responding to his knock, she opened the door to him the following afternoon. She was wearing a silk wrap not fully covering a black bra and black silk panties.

'Flying visit,' he said, placing a small paper bag on the bureau.

'Oh.' Damn.

'Phoned your mother yet?'

'I can't get through.'

'Well, I'm not fucking you until we've made the announcement and I can legitimately move back in here. I want to take you in my bed.'

'Really? Whatever happened to the kitchen table?'

'I can do both. I'm versatile.'

'So am I.' She reached down for him.

He knocked her hand away.

'Oh dear. Don't tell me you're worried you're too small.'

He laughed, spun her round and slapped her bottom. 'You won't be disappointed. Anyway, I've got something else to show you.'

He crossed to the bureau and handed her the paper bag. She saw it was from the photographic shop. Inside, she found an oval silver frame containing the photo he had taken of her at the top of Cannes. He must have had it developed express.

'I'll put it on the piano with all the others,' he said. 'No one will notice.'

Constanza will, Paula thought. When she's dusting.

Patric paused at the door, running his eyes over her bronzed curves. 'Try your mother again.'

It was early evening. It was the big one. It was the day, Liz and Kit had decided, he must propose to Ilona.

The romance had been put on hold during the period when Joleen was kidnapped. Now they had to push on. Liz didn't want Patric realizing that Ilona had the hots for Kit and moving in to put the damper on it.

While the men were away rescuing Joleen, Liz had taken Patric's car and reconnoitred suitable proposal sites. Up on the Moyen Corniche, towards the perched village of Èze, she'd found it. Kit and Ilona could get out of the Daimler, walk a little way and look down on Villefranche, one of the most lyrical bays on the planet. It would be sunset. Poetic. Perfect.

As long as Kit didn't screw up. He had refused to rehearse what he was going to say. And he had refused to take the ring. 'Too contrived. Why would I come on holiday with a ring? I'll produce it in a few days' time, as if I've just bought it.'

From her bedroom window Liz watched them leave. Ilona was wearing a dress of forget-me-not blue. Liz said to Golly, 'He's getting too independent. I don't like it.'

On her way downstairs she heard Paula running a bath. She was singing.

Liz retreated to the top-floor bathroom. Paula was singing some stupid song by Alma Cogan:

> Sugar in the mornin', sugar in the evenin',
> Sugar at supper time.
> Be my little sugar,
> I'll love you all the time.

But over the singing, from somewhere downstairs, Liz thought she heard a weird noise, an animal in pain, that seemed to echo her own anguish.

Then it stopped. She washed her face. Sprayed on scent. Had a brisk talk with herself. You are not going to howl. You look like a jam puff when you cry. You and Kit are within an ace of pulling this off. And there's no going back. She wants him. She'll have him.

It was three hours before the Daimler swept back up the drive. The wait, having supper on the terrace, had seemed interminable.

Liz had listened to Paula telling Patric about the extraordinary change in Joleen. 'We were so worried about her. She was putrid to Colin. I'm surprised he put up with it.'

He didn't, Liz informed her silently. He wanted me. It may surprise you to know, Paula dear, that lots of men have fancied me. But I have only ever loved Kit.

'Of course, it helps that the cystitis has cleared up,' Paula was saying, 'but I think there's something else.'

Patric nodded. He had run into Colin near the photographic shop this morning and thought that, for a man with serious financial problems, Colin was looking remarkably cheerful.

*

Liz watched Kit get out of the Daimler. He walked round to the passenger door and opened it for Ilona. Gracefully, she got out of the car.

They walked up towards the terrace. They were holding hands. Halfway, they stopped. Ilona looked into his eyes, and murmured something. He smiled that slow, amused smile, and kissed her, lightly.

Liz took a great slug of wine.

Kit had swung it.

At the foot of the table the couple paused. Kit had his arm round her waist. It was as if they couldn't let one another go. Ever.

'You tell them.'

'No, you tell them.'

Paula leaped up. 'You two! You're engaged!'

'Oh my God,' said Patric.

'How lovely,' gushed Liz. 'Congratulations, both of you.'

'You don't congratulate the woman. Just the man,' Paula told her, but in such a mild tone that Liz was instantly suspicious. What with that and warbling sugary songs in the bath . . . it had to be a man. Patric. Was it all on again? Better keep an eye on them.

'Champagne,' Patric was saying, 'And we'll phone the boat. Get the Loves round here.'

In the grand salon Kit and Liz rolled up the Aubusson and ferried it away into the dining-room. Patric produced a box of imported LPs. He placed it next to the walnut stereogram and appointed Paula officer-in-charge of music.

She pouted. 'If I'm changing records all night I won't be able to dance as much.'

'I can't dance with you until I've fucked you. I'd go mad.'

She opened the box. Concentrated. Oh great. Oh boy! He'd got Elvis, Buddy Holly, Chris Barber. That would do to start. She put on 'Petite Fleur' as Patric opened the champagne and Joleen hurtled in.

'Ilona! How did he propose? What did he say?'

Just what I want to know, thought Liz sourly.

Ilona smiled across at Kit. 'What did he say? He just said yes. I asked him.'

'That's funny. I proposed to Colin. I said, "Col, we'd better get married." Didn't I, Col?'

Colin sat on the leather sofa. He couldn't believe how his life had started anew, couldn't believe the sea change that had come over Joleen.

'We must lead a simpler life, Colin,' she had said. 'We've just got so much stuff we don't need. The yacht. We only use it twice a year. The London house. What do we need that for? I prefer New York.'

'But your London friends. Lady Kilmartin –'

'Her! That woman. You know what, Col, she called me common!'

Colin hugged her and thought, Christ, oh Christ, she's back. The old Joleen. The one. The original. His wife, his woman. She was back.

Over by the long window Ilona was telling Joleen about her row with Patric after he had seen her swimming naked. He had told her to cover up.

'It's not fair to the pool boy. He's fifteen. You're thirty. To fifteen thirty is ancient.'

'He probably thought you fancied the boy,' said Joleen.

'Come off it. Why would I fancy a fifteen-year-old?'

Oh, I don't know, thought Joleen. She remembered Guido meticulously, under her instruction, cutting the red dress at her knees. The scissors in his right hand. His left hand steady on her thigh.

That morning the big captor had untied her and told her they would leave her on the main road. When she said she wasn't going he shrugged and went and started the Lambretta.

'I am staying here,' Joleen said to Guido. She eased off her wedding ring, put it into his trouser pocket and pointed at his sandals. 'I buy those?'

The boy nodded. He took off his sandals, kneeled down and fitted them on her. Then he took out her ring and, still kneeling, slipped it back on her finger.

She looked for the last time at his slender fingers, his long dark lashes, his sensitive mouth. She couldn't stop herself. She bent and kissed him on that mouth, with a tenderness that astounded both of them.

Seated by the stereo, Paula was enjoying herself planning her phone call to Ben, her now very ex-boyfriend. Dare she invite him to the wedding? Poor taste? Anyway Patric was bound to veto it.

Under cover of Anthony Newley, Patric said to Paula, 'You suit my house. Will you be happy living here?'

Would she!

'Of course, it'll be *your* house. You're the woman. Change what you want.'

She was ahead of him there. The striped dining-room curtains, for a start, would have to go.

'At one time you might have had Edward and Mrs Simpson as neighbours. They were going to buy a house in Cannes...'

They were watching Kit dancing with his fiancée. Radiant is the only word for her, thought Paula. And dear Kit. Proud and amazed all at the same time.

As the dance finished Ilona said something to Kit, and he went straight across to where Lizzie was sitting, hunched near the piano.

'Miss Clarke, you didn't do me the honour at the last party.'

He pulled her up. Paula put on Eddie Cochran, 'C'mon Everybody', and Liz and Kit hit the floor. No one but Kit had seen Liz dance before. Ilona had gone to get another glass of water, so she didn't notice. But everyone else thought, Goodness, just look how those two jive. Who would have believed it? Joleen's yellow eyes went into slits. It was as if they'd been dancing together all their lives.

At the end of the record Liz murmured, 'Go on. You can do it. You've had enough booze to do it.'

He went into the kitchen and returned with the large Italian pepper mill. 'Can you put on Lloyd Price?' he asked Paula. '"Stagger Lee".'

So with the pepper mill as a mike, and Lloyd Price leading, Kit launched into a raunchily hilarious impression of a rock-'n'-roll singer.

'Come on, Paula,' yelled Joleen. 'We're the backing group. Get clapping and shift that ass!'

Skirts swirling, they let go and gave it their all. All three of them were so sensational Ilona was crying with laughter. At the stereo she said, 'Encore', and put on 'There'll Never Be Anyone Else But You'. Assisted by Ricky Nelson, Kit sang it straight to Ilona, with Paula and Joleen crooning away beside him.

Patric was watching Liz's face. Her eyes were bright with unshed tears. Poor kid, he thought. Poor Lizzie.

He got Kit a beer, and they flopped on the sofa. 'You do know,' Patric said, nodding towards Ilona, 'there's no immediate fortune.'

He's either totally pissed or he's lost his marbles, thought Kit. He grinned at the older man. 'Actually, I think she's after *my* money.'

Patric called across to Ilona. 'Tell me. The evacuee line-up. Why did you choose Paula?'

'Because I saw her punch the boy next to her.'

Paula flung a cushion at her. 'Cheek! He pinched me first.'

Kit tapped Joleen on the shoulder. 'I know what I meant to tell you. You got off lightly with those pretty little mauve jellyfish. Off Japan the jellies are the size of a washing-machine.'

'You're kidding.'

'The Chinese eat jellies,' said Paula. 'With sesame oil and onions.'

'Personally,' said Colin, 'I prefer my jelly with custard.'

Time for bed, decided a thoroughly miserable Liz. She slipped away, with the night's top song beating in her head: 'A Fool Such As I'.

SIXTEEN

LIZ SLID INTO Kit's bed the next morning and woke him the way he liked best. These trysts had got to stop. She accepted that. Ilona might decide to come and wake him herself, might wonder what on earth Liz was doing in his room, let alone his bed.

He was awake.

Liz demanded, 'What did she say when she asked you to marry her?'

He took a sip of water. 'That's private. That's her and me.'

Liz felt like biting him. But they'd agreed. No marks. Not now.

She said furiously, 'Why were you so long? What did she do? Did she go down on you?'

'No. Actually I get the feeling she doesn't sort of know about that.'

'What happened then?'

'We got back in the car. Kissed a lot and – um – petted.'

'What did you do?'

He sighed. 'Unbuttoned her dress. Played with her – very small – breasts.'

'Did you get in her knickers?'

'No. Had the sense not to try.'

'Listen. Where's the golly?'

'What?'

'The golly. The golly I sewed the ring into. Where is it?'

'I haven't got it. You had it. Near your bed.'

'Well, it's gone. I thought you'd taken it when you came back from Èze.'

'No.'

She threw on some clothes and hurried to the kitchen. Constanza was clearing up after the party. Liz explained about the missing golly. Had Constanza perhaps moved it when she turned out the bedrooms?

Constanza rested on her broom. 'I no move the doll. But Marie-Laure, she came again to find the kittens. She so upset there no kittens, Mr Ryan, he go fetch the doll and he give it to Marie-Laure.'

While Liz was digesting this, thinking vengefully, 'Marie-Laure if you just knew where that golly had been,' Ilona came in from the pool. She was wearing a demure one-piece bathing dress with a frilled skirt.

'This is all for that prude Patric's benefit,' she told Liz. 'The skirt's horrible. Feels all clammy when it's wet.' She poured herself some orange juice. 'Anyway best knickers today, Lizzie. We're all going shopping for our wedding outfits.'

Liz took a step back. 'No, I –'

'No buts,' said Ilona. 'This is my *wedding*. Of course you must have something new. My treat. And, don't worry, I won't let them intimidate you.'

Chez Gervaise was the most exclusive establishment on one of the most exclusive shopping streets in the world – the rue d'Antibes in Cannes. It featured one dress in the window, in cream shantung displayed against pleated panels of dark-green silk. The panels were artfully arranged so that the quartet of friends on the pavement could not see the interior of the shop. But Madame Gervaise and her assistant were afforded a clear view of the street.

'The blonde one, I will dress,' Madame Gervaise informed her assistant. 'And the petite brunette and the one with the strange eyes. But the fat one I will not dress.'

'But, Madame –'

'No! I will not dress the fat one. She would ruin my reputation!'

Gowned from head to foot in black, she positioned herself in the middle of her establishment, and, as Ilona swept in with the others, she assumed her customary selling expression of total disdain.

Liz watched Ilona and Paula exchange a we're-not-standing-for-this look. Joleen for once had the sense to keep her trap shut.

Speaking in English, in a cut-glass accent Liz could see Madame was having difficulty understanding, Ilona explained what she wanted. A wedding outfit, but, no, not white or ivory. She wanted pink. Very, very pale pink. A nice pink. 'Not,' Ilona said, regarding the woman of a certain age she was addressing, 'not an old-woman pink.'

Madame Gervaise smiled stiffly and rapped at her assistant, 'Make a note. The Italian silk.'

'Yes, Madame.' Oh, this was delicious! She couldn't wait to tell her girlfriends over lunch.

Ilona indicated Paula. 'Miss Montgomery has kindly consented to be my bridesmaid. Now in terms of colour for her, I –'

'Ice green,' interrupted Madame Gervaise, realizing it was time she regained control. 'She has olive skin. She should wear ice green.'

There was an awkward pause. None of them had the foggiest what ice green was.

Liz muttered hesitantly, 'Did she say ice cream?'

'No!' Paula exclaimed. 'Ice green. Of course!' She gave Madame Gervaise a conspiratorial smile. 'How inspirational. How *chic*. You are thinking . . . you are thinking *sorbet*.'

Madame Gervaise had been thinking nothing of the sort. She'd been flying a kite. But now her imagination soared. 'Exact! I am thinking fresh, I am thinking cool and so, so pretty.' She turned to Joleen. 'For you, the palest lemon. And for your friend,' Madame Gervaise ignored the smirk of her assistant, 'vanilla. Charming.'

'Vanilla?' queried Joleen. 'Isn't that cream? People will think she's the bride.'

'Good. It's fun to confuse people,' said Ilona. 'You never know, Lizzie. You might get to marry Kit.'

Oh, the mirth, thought Liz, as Madame semaphored to the assistant that she should go and be measured. Now they're wondering if they've got a tape measure big enough.

'You English, you always have such lovely skin,' the assistant said to Liz as she led her away. 'We envy you so much.'

'The only problem is,' Ilona was telling Madame, 'the wedding is on Friday. So you've only got five days.'

'That is not too serious. We have our own *atelier*. We will work round the clock.'

Kneeling in front of Liz in the *cabine* the assistant's smile faded. No lunch with the girls then. Not for days and days and days.

'And may I ask, Madame, you are getting married in Cannes?'

'No. I'm getting married on Mrs Love's yacht.'

They went over the details at the bistro under the linden trees. As captain and a qualified yachtmaster, Knut was empowered to conduct burials, christenings and weddings at sea.

'We have to be outside French territorial waters,' said Joleen. 'But that's no problem.'

Ilona had refused to be given away. Both Patric and Colin had offered.

'Thanks, but no. I wasn't given away the first time either, because my father had disowned me.'

They were waiting for Kit and Patric. There had been some debate this morning about what the groom was going to wear. Morning dress seemed too formal for a yacht wedding. White would make him look too much like Knut. Finally they decided he should have a dove-grey silk suit, white shirt and grey silk tie.

'I'll take you along to my tailor,' Patric said. 'Have to be off the peg at this short notice. Ilona, do you think Kit will look all right with an Italian cut to the jacket?'

'Oh, my Kit can wear anything.'

Liz left the table.

'Italian?' repeated Kit. 'I don't want to look like a Mod!'

'Don't be daft,' said Ilona. 'This is *Patric's* tailor.'

Before the men arrived at the restaurant Ilona told them that Kit wanted the honeymoon to be in London.

'What a good idea,' said Liz.

'He is sweet. You know, he won't make love to me until the wedding night.'

Good, thought Paula. That makes two of us not getting it. She was planning to buy Kit a silver cigarette case as a wedding present. Ilona wouldn't approve, but, hell, did they have to do what Ilona said all the time?

'He wanted to buy me an engagement ring, but I said would he mind if I had a new wedding ring but carried on wearing the one from Hans as well.'

They talked about the flowers. Deep-pink roses for Ilona, cream for Paula. Kit would have one of Ilona's roses in his buttonhole. 'Look good on the grey silk. Oh, here they are.'

It seemed the most natural thing in the world for Kit to walk straight up to Ilona and kiss her. It nearly broke Lizzie's heart.

'I thought Colin was coming,' Patric said to Joleen.

'No. Busy. Some new scheme he won't tell me about yet.'

Last night, in bed, she'd whispered a confession.

'Col, you know when they tied my hands? Hey, it was – exciting. You know?'

'You didn't –'

'No! But listen' . . . She told him what she wanted, what he was to go and buy . . . 'And I don't want rough old hand-cuffs. I want pink ones, velvet-lined.'

Colin protested that he didn't know where to go for frilly handcuffs.

'There'll be a shop near the station, Colin. There always is. There'll be a photo of some dame running through the surf, and the shop will be called something like Health and Efficiency. You'll find it.'

After lunch Kit and Ilona went to buy the ring. Joleen asked Liz to walk back with her to the *Lovebite*. 'We ought to think about a wedding present.'

So Paula travelled back with Patric, Kit's suit, four hat boxes and four new pairs of gloves.

'The reason you can't get hold of your mother is that her mother is in hospital and your mother is staying near by,' Patric said. 'Nothing serious. She just didn't want to worry you.'

'How . . . ?' But Paula knew how. Mrs bloody Armstrong. She said, 'When did you realize you wanted to marry me?'

'When I first set eyes on you. In Fortnum's. You came in with this slow, almost insolent walk. As if you owned the place and really couldn't care less.'

'My shoes were sopping. I couldn't walk fast.'

'You were magnificent.' He put on the handbrake and touched her face. 'I love you, Paula.'

'There's no one in,' Paula said hopefully. 'It's Constanza's afternoon off.'

'No,' he said. 'Let's wait. We'll tell them our news towards the end of the wedding party. Kit and Ilona are going to Eden Roc for the night. We'll leave Lizzie on the boat. Then I can bring you home and carry you over the threshold.'

SEVENTEEN

'THE DRESSES! WHERE are they?' Liz heard Ilona scream. 'They should be here by now!'

Liz turned over in bed. Natural for Ilona to be in a state. Actually, she sounded more than tense. She sounded completely overwrought.

'Paula! Call the shop.'

'You call the shop. It's your fucking wedding.'

Oh dear. Liz hauled herself out of bed. There had been one last embrace with Kit in his bed last night.

Liz, in tears, as he kissed her and said, 'I love you, Lizzie. Never forget, I love *you.*'

Now she left her bedroom and prepared to face what she knew, without doubt, would be the worst day of her life.

The wedding was to take place at eleven thirty.

'No point in doing it later,' Patric had said. 'Everyone hanging around getting nervous.' And drinking too much.

The florist's van arrived at seven thirty. 'Scented roses!' exclaimed Paula. 'They're quite hard to get. All the best ones go to Grasse.'

Constanza came out from the kitchen to the terrace and handed Ilona a small sprig of a green plant. 'It is *myrte*.'

'Myrtle,' translated Paula.

'Yes,' said Constanza. 'It is lucky for you to put it in your flowers. After the wedding you plant it in your garden. If it grows, your marriage is good.'

It was a classic Côte d'Azur blue-sky day, but already Paula could hear the wind in the palms. The sea might be choppy. She said to Liz, 'Did you get those seasickness pills? I should take one now.'

It was eight o'clock. Madame Gervaise's white Mercedes was proceeding up the drive. She was alone, as the assistant had taken Joleen's dress to the boat.

At this moment, Kit arrived on the terrace. He was dressed for his wedding. Liz had never in her life felt such agony. He looked so handsome. She loved him so much.

'No!' yelled Constanza, shoving herself between him and Ilona. 'You cannot see her. It is bad luck to see the girl before the wedding.'

'Superstitious bunk,' scoffed Ilona. She took one of the deep pink roses from her bouquet and slipped it into Kit's buttonhole.

'And I mustn't forget to put this on,' she said, unwrapping the blue garter the girls had given her. 'I'm glad we agreed, no other presents. It's not as if we need anything, Kit, is it?'

Speak for your bloody self, he thought. There's rather a lot I want, actually.

Liz saw Madame Gervaise eyeing him with approval. He looked attractively fit, poised, ready.

He's accepted it, this marriage, Liz realized. He's grown into the part. Now I have to as well. Can't let him down.

Patric, to Madame Gervaise's amazement, took a photo of a sullen Ilona lounging on the terrace, morning gown open, showing off the garter. Then the women went upstairs to Ilona's room.

Madame Gervaise propelled Liz forward. 'We dress you first.'

Madame had pulled out all the stops for this, the most challenging client of her entire career. The vanilla dress was of silk taffeta, which gave it structure and which was cleverly cut to skim the hips.

Liz looked at herself in the mirror and realized that never before had she seemed so glamorous. She felt a complete dream. 'Thank you,' she whispered. 'Thank you so much.'

Meanwhile Paula was attempting to do Ilona's hair and makeup.

'I don't want any powder,' snapped the bride. 'I never wear powder.'

'It's just to take away the shine for the photographs,' Paula said, puff in hand. She wondered if she had ever seen Ilona in such a state.

At last, when Madame had dressed Paula, Ilona stood in her stockings and pants in the middle of the room. Madame advanced with the dress and slipped it over Ilona's head. The bra had been sewn in, so this was hooked up first. The pale pink Italian silk was gorgeous, perfectly plain, except that at the fitting, when Madame had learned of her deep-pink bouquet, she had decalled the hem and had sewn in just a few tiny deep-pink silk roses to harmonize with the scented flowers.

Finally, the hats. Madame had counselled small hats so their faces would show well in the photographs. Firmly, she pinned them on. Then she kissed Ilona on each cheek. 'Good luck, Madame.'

Ilona descended the stairs first. Kit and Patric were waiting at the bottom, Patric wearing a navy blazer and white trousers. As Ilona reached the last stair Kit took her hand, raised it to his lips and kissed it. Then he whispered something in her ear that brought, at last, a smile to the bride's face.

Patric said to Paula, 'That's an interesting colour on you. With your eyes I always think of you in blue.'

'Oh, I'm versatile,' Paula flashed back. Blue eyes met blue. They were both thinking of later. Oh, how she wanted later!

Patric put his hand on Kit's shoulder. 'All set?'

'All set.'

Patric and Kit left the house with Liz. A Mercedes would be arriving shortly to take Paula and the bride.

At the Daimler Kit automatically went to get in the driver's seat.

Patric took the keys from him. 'I don't think so, old man. Not today.'

In the back of the car Liz was glaring at Kit's back. What had he said to Ilona on the stairs? What had he *said*?

Knut, Joleen and Colin were waiting on the yacht to greet them. Joleen's pale-lemon dress was of finely pleated silk. Apart from her wedding ring and watch she was wearing no jewellery.

'I know what you're thinking,' she laughed to Liz, 'but we're poor now. Haven't you heard? Isn't it wonderful?'

She's deranged, thought Liz. Everyone's potty today. Thank heavens for Knut.

He was lining up the entire crew on the side of the boat facing the quay. They were all in their smartly pressed uniform, and Knut was resplendent in his dress whites.

'Got the ring, Colin?' asked Patric.

Colin patted his breast pocket. 'Trust me.'

He led the way into the salon, which Joleen, at Ilona's request, had massed with pure white flowers. Colin took a Bloody Mary from the bar steward's tray and handed it to Kit. 'Get this down you.'

Actually, thought Liz, it's me that needs a strong drink. She took one. Practically ate it. Checked her watch. Just after ten thirty. Ilona was late.

By five to eleven Kit had cracked and lit a cigarette. What Patric hadn't wanted to happen was happening. Everyone standing around shaky with nerves and hitting the booze.

'We've got to get out of French waters before the ceremony,' Colin said to Liz. 'So we're running late. Can't be helped. Have a drink.'

'Thanks.'

'They're coming,' Knut announced.

He went alone on to the deck. As Ilona descended from the Mercedes he gave a command and the entire crew snapped to attention. Ilona gracefully ascended the gangway. Knut saluted and assisted her aboard.

Paula was four steps behind. Knut escorted them to the flower bower of a salon, then went to the bridge to await orders from Colin.

Ilona and Paula stood together at the entrance to the salon. Paula looks ghastly, thought Liz. The sea is choppy, but actually I don't think that green colour really suits her. And just see Ilona, pale and grave, a dead spit of Grace Kelly on her wedding day. Incredible what could happen in an hour. One minute you were a Hollywood actress, pursuing everything in sight. Then sixty minutes in church, one wedding ring and, hey presto, you were a Princess, a Serene Highness, with streets and a hospital named after you.

Joleen was standing next to Colin, who was beside Kit at the far end of the salon. There's something not right, thought Joleen. But what? I just can't figure it.

All eyes were on the bride. Ilona walked alone the length of the salon and went up to Kit. She took his hands in hers.

'Kit, dear. I'm sorry. I'm so, so sorry. But I can't marry you.'

Suddenly Joleen got it. The flowers. Neither Ilona nor Paula were carrying their bouquets.

Colin had his arm round the bride. 'Look, everyone gets last-minute nerves.'

She shrugged him off. Kept her eyes on Kit. 'I was wrong to ask you, Kit.'

The women sat down. The men cleared their throats. Liz burst into tears. Joleen called to the bar steward for more drinks. Colin sent a message to Knut to stand the crew down.

'Is it Hans?' said Joleen. 'Are you still in love with him?'

'Yes, but it's more than that. I'm having his baby.'

Kit was wondering what the hell to do, what to say. What were you supposed to say when the woman pulled out of your wedding? What was the etiquette? Surely he wasn't supposed to say, 'Oh let's get married anyway, and what a privilege for me to bring up sodding Hans's kid.'

But no one was paying any attention to him. They were firing questions at Ilona.

Finally Paula tried to take charge. 'I think it's easier if I explain. Ilona's had a dreadful morning. She needs to rest.'

'I'm not ill, Paula. I'm just pregnant.'

Paula, in whom Ilona had confided only that morning, gave them some details. Ilona's last holiday with Hans, when they went to Switzerland, had been like a honeymoon. The child was conceived then. Ilona was now three-and-a-half months pregnant.

'How did you find out you were pregnant? Surely you must have known?'

'No. Didn't occur to me. The curse has always been irregular with me. Then Constanza saw me getting out of the pool with nothing on. The last time before Patric stopped me. She said, "Madame, we need to go to the doctor." I didn't know what she was talking about, so I didn't. Then she kept on and on about babies. I thought she was mad, but I went. By now the wedding was all planned, and

I just didn't know what to do. So I thought, I'll just wait for the results. They take ages.'

'You don't speak French,' said Joleen. 'How did you manage at the doctor's?'

'Constanza came with me. Then they rang up with the results. This morning. After you'd gone.'

By now Kit had got the script straight in his head. He knew what to do.

He went over to Ilona and said, still standing, 'Ilona, I'm delighted you're happy. I felt very honoured when you – when you chose me. But you have to follow your heart. Believe me, I understand that.' He bent and kissed her and walked out on to the deck.

The women sat speechless in sheer admiration. Liz saw Patric and Colin exchange a glance. Yes, agreed Liz. Wasn't that so dignified? So manly. So unforgettable.

As Joleen ordered canapés to be brought, Ilona said she knew it would be difficult, but she wanted to bring up Hans's child on her own.

Patric intervened. 'You won't be on your own. You have us. Live at the villa if you like. You never know. There might be other babies coming along.'

He was looking straight at Paula. She wished she was wearing a wide-brimmed hat. She was doing something she wished she could grow out of. Blushing.

Patric pulled her up beside him. 'You may not be getting married, Ilona, but Paula and I are. Very soon.'

Crikey, thought Liz. This is even better than *The Archers*.

What happens now? wondered Kit, out on deck. All togged up to get married, and now you're not. The Plan, obviously, is cancelled forthwith.

He felt Colin's hand on the shoulder of his new suit.

'Tough day, Kit.'

'Yep.'

'Look, Patric and I, we thought, no point hanging round here. Shall we go for a spin? We could drop Lizzie off on the way.'

Later, in the Mercedes on the way back to the villa, Paula said to Ilona, 'What do you really feel for Kit?'

'Well, I fancy him. I mean, who wouldn't? But I was never in love with him. I love Hans. There can never be anyone else. We wanted children desperately, but it just never happened. Then when I got to the villa – I didn't know I was pregnant, obviously – when I saw Kit I thought, wow, genetically we can't go wrong. It was selfish, asking him to marry me so he could be the father of my child.'

She tore off her pillbox hat. 'But he must never know the truth, Paula. He must always think I loved him dearly but that the memory of Hans was just too strong.'

'Of course.' Paula followed suit and unpinned her hat. 'I don't understand why you kept all this to yourself. I could have come with you to the doctor. You didn't need to involve Constanza.'

'It just happened that way. And, in any case, you have been a bit away with the fairies, you know.'

Patric. Last seen gliding away in the Daimler with Colin and Kit. 'I wonder what Kit will do now. Go back to England, I suppose.'

'I really feel upset about Kit. Embarrassing him. In front of all our friends. You know, when I came downstairs this morning, he whispered to me, "I love you to distraction."'

'Oh God. Poor guy.'

'I was wondering . . . I could ask Patric to release some of my money. I could give Kit a cheque. A sort of thank-you-and-I'm-sorry present.'

'Give him money?' echoed Paula. 'Oh no. Quite the wrong thing. Kit's a gentleman. He'd be deeply offended.'

Maybe you're right, thought Ilona. But I'm going to do it anyway.

Paula spent the afternoon alone, sunbathing by the pool. She was reading *Bonjour Tristesse* and wearing a shocking-pink bikini. The novel was bitter-sweet of course, but there was nothing Paula enjoyed more than a sad story when she herself felt totally carefree.

At six she came indoors. The door of her room, which she had locked, was open. Patric was there. He was unpacking his things. Rapidly taking possession.

She stood in the doorway. He said, 'I saw your face when Ilona was talking about Hans and the baby. You looked so delighted for her. I knew he really was all over for you.'

Paula didn't move. 'In Fortnum's I can appreciate that you might have fancied me. But why did you want to marry me?'

'Because I realized you were the sort of woman who should be taken off the streets.'

'Streets? You make me sound like a tart!'

He slung his leather holdall under the bed. 'Well, you know what they say about a wife being a whore in the bedroom.'

'It's time for cocktails,' she said, as he came towards her. 'I have to get changed.'

'Good. Allow me to assist you.'

He slipped down the straps of her bikini, pulled her into the room and kicked the door firmly shut.

'They want you to do *what*?' demanded Liz.

She and Kit were in her bed. As usual, it was a squash. It made her long for their own double bed. There wasn't much you could say about East Croydon, but the bedsit was huge and the bed itself was always welcoming.

Now Kit was telling her about Colin's insane idea. He wanted to turn Kit into a rock singer. Colin and Joleen would be the management team. He'd got the idea when he saw Kit doing his party piece, rocking along with the pepper mill.

'But Joleen. Muscling in. You know she controls Colin. You don't like Joleen.'

'No, she's a pain in the arse. She's more relaxed these days, but you know, leopard . . . spots. But the thing is, in a manager, being a pain in the bum is an asset. Patric was telling me. He's got a client who does the Palladium, all that. You've got to have someone tough, fighting for money, the right lighting, the best crew. One thing about having Joleen at your shoulder – she won't take any shit.'

'She doesn't know anything about the music business. Neither does Colin.'

'They didn't know fast food either when they started.'

'But you can't sing,' protested Liz. 'You can only do it if you sing along to someone who can sing.'

'I know. I told Colin. He said it was fine, lots of the rock lot have no voice at all. You just get a mixed backing group who *can* sing and make a lot of noise, and away you go.'

Liz turned over. 'What does Patric think?'

'He thinks it's a great idea. Especially me being the son of an earl. Terrific publicity. My sister-in-law will go berserk. I can't wait.' Kit sat up. 'Anyway, that wasn't all. Colin asked if I could play the guitar, and I said no, but I could pretend. You know what he said? He said, "Sunshine, the amount of pretending you've been doing lately, looks like we should turn you into a rocking actor."'

Liz felt all clammy. 'You mean he *knows*?'

'Yep. Joleen. Female instinct.'

'What did Patric say?'

'Oh, he's known for ages apparently. He's got some secretary fancies herself as a private dick.'

He's been playing with us, Liz thought. Perhaps he
would have stepped in and stopped the wedding. I can
understand him wanting to thwart us, but why do that to
Ilona? To an old friend and a valued client?

'Kit, I thought you wanted to live in La Bocca. A dear little
house . . . A dog.'

'We could still have that. Be a nice base to come back to.'

'But what about me? While you and Colin and Joleen are
off rocking and touring, what am I supposed to do?'

'You'd be with me. I mean, with all those hysterical girl
fans I'd be safer with my wife by my side.'

She fell back on the pillow. 'Kit, you never wanted to be
married.'

'No, and I very nearly was, to Ilona. I just want to make
quite sure you don't put me through anything like this
again. I couldn't stand it.'

When Kit had dropped Colin at the boat and he and
Patric were driving to the villa, Patric said, 'Can I suggest
that you and Liz disappear off the map for a while. Then
we'll put it about that you fell for Liz on the rebound. The
point is, I don't want Ilona hurt. She must always think you
are carrying a torch for her.'

Kit didn't report this conversation to his new fiancée. He
was learning not to burden Lizzie with everything.

Perhaps it was called growing up. On the other hand, he
reasoned, was that really a good plan? Was there any such
thing as a grown-up rock star?

Also published by Peter Owen

CASSANDRA'S DISK
Angela Green

978 0 7206 1144 1 • paperback • 260pp • £10.95

'She's very, very good. An excellent novel. I'm always wanting to come across a new writer who completely engrosses with their art, and she is one.' – Alan Sillitoe

'A metafictional puzzle, Borges-style . . . The twist in the novel's tail makes the point: there can be no such thing as truth in human relations, nor indeed in a work of fiction.' – *Times Literary Supplement*

In a white, cell-like room on the Greek island of Ithaca, photographer Cassandra Byrd – giantess, eccentric, sexual siren and twin – races to fill her computer disk with a raucous account of her highly unprincipled past.

Aware that her twin sister Helen had been born with a double share of beauty, calcium, talent and maternal love, the young Cassandra reinvented herself as the vulgar, uninhibited 'Big Bad Baby'. When Helen survives their catastrophic childhood to become a successful actress, Cassandra sets out on a rampaging odyssey through New York, London and Paris, secretly following her sister's sexual trail in order to prove her own attractiveness.

www.peterowen.com

Peter Owen books can be purchased from:
Central Books, 99 Wallis Road, London E9 5LN, UK
Tel: +44 (0) 845 458 9911 Fax: + 44 (0) 845 458 9912
e-mail: orders@centralbooks.com

Also published by Peter Owen

THE COLOUR OF WATER
Angela Green
978 0 7206 1204 2 • paperback • 224pp • £11.95

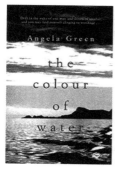

'An evocative, artfully structured exploration of the mysteries of identity and the journey back from disillusionment to hope.' – *Kirkus Reviews*

'An exceptionally clever, vivacious account of sibling rivalry . . .' – *Spectator*

'An excellent writer whose characters live . . . impossible to put down.' – *newBOOKSmag*

Anna Larssen drifted for years in the wake of one man and the dream of another and awoke to find herself clinging to the wreckage. Her illusions shattered, she leaves her home in France and travels to an island at the northern rim of the world, to a place called, simply, A.

Beneath the Norwegian Lofoten peaks, as she struggles to disentangle the fact and fiction of her life, Anna remembers the enigmatic Resistance hero she married and the mysterious American she briefly loved; but in resurrecting the past, she summons up more than mere ghosts of memory.

www.peterowen.com

Peter Owen books can be purchased from:
Central Books, 99 Wallis Road, London E9 5LN, UK
Tel: +44 (0) 845 458 9911 Fax: + 11 (0) 845 458 9912
e-mail: orders@centralbooks.com

Also published by Peter Owen

LYING
Wendy Perriam

978 0 7206 1128 1 • paperback • 304pp • £7.99

'An accomplished and intelligent novel by a too often overlooked novelist who wears her seriousness of purpose lightly.' – *Independent*

'She gets to the heart of the matter, and there, lurking beneath the seriously mundane, we discover the spiritual underpinnings of the universe.' – Fay Weldon

Alison is asked to read an important manuscript over the weekend, courting disaster when she picks up the wrong briefcase on the train. It belongs to Cambridge-educated accountant, James: lean, handsome, virginal and *ultra* Catholic. After a single meeting Alison falls obsessively in love and, desperate to attract him, reinvents herself as a Catholic.

She marries into his formidable family, but after five years of marriage finds herself compelled to lead a double life, upholding 'truths' in public which she privately abhors. The strain of this deception leads her into an affair. Yet she still loves James and respects his deeply held faith. Hence her profound shock upon discovering that even James is entangled in a web of deceptions.

www.peterowen.com

Peter Owen books can be purchased from:
Central Books, 99 Wallis Road, London E9 5LN, UK
Tel: +44 (0) 845 458 9911 Fax: + 11 (0) 845 458 9912
e-mail: orders@centralbooks.com